LOVE IN THE DETAILS

CHRISTMAS AT THE MANSION

BRITNEY M. MILLS

CRYSTAL CANYON PUBLISHING

CHAPTER 1

The tension in Kassidy McBride's stomach had reached astronomical heights. She checked the clock on the wall across from her, the seconds ticking by as she tried to avoid looking at the door to her right. Her coworker, Tanya, had been in there nearly fifteen minutes already. Did that mean she was getting the promotion from bank teller to loan officer? Or was Trace Bentley, branch manager for the Coldwater Creek Bank and ex-boyfriend to Kassidy, merely letting her down easy?

Kassidy had been working toward that promotion for the last eight months, ever since she'd come back to the valley after a short four-month stint in LA. The fact that she'd had to work under her ex-boyfriend hadn't been all peaches and roses, but she'd survived up until this point. She'd even managed to keep her mouth shut a time or two.

She entered her information in the browser and saw the balance in her bank account. If she got this promotion, she'd finally be able to afford a place of her own. Her family was amazing, but she could do with more space. At twenty-five, it was high time.

Her two oldest brothers had married within the last year, leaving her twin brothers and younger sister, Molly, all in the same house together, which didn't exactly bring the independence she'd been searching for in LA. Then again, she was searching for some kind of direction to take her life. Ever since she'd decided to retire from barrel racing, she hadn't been able to get a win in anything she did. The only bonus about that was the comfort of her own bed night after night instead of the constant travel to one rodeo after another.

Tanya Roberts walked out of the boss's office, her expression smug as she stared at Kassidy.

The young blonde walked over to Elaina, the teller at the desk next to Kassidy's, and said with a quick glance in Kassidy's direction, "I got the promotion!"

Of course she had. Of all days to award a promotion, Black Friday was not a day Kassidy had expected. She was still wishing she was home, hoping her brothers didn't eat all of the leftover turkey.

She blew out a breath, again focusing on the clock on the wall across from her. As much as Kassidy had hoped for that little pay increase and something different as far as work responsibilities, she should have known Trace would never bump her up to a position where he would have to work more closely with her. Breaking up with someone because she needed a change and then coming back months later, groveling for her old job back, didn't shine a good light on her character.

Pulling out a stress ball stamped with the bank's logo on the side, Kassidy focused on the screen, squeezing the ball in an attempt to avoid punching the girl in the face. Coldwater Creek was a small town, and the last thing she wanted was word to spread that she'd started a fight.

The fact that Tanya had only started working there five

months ago dug at Kassidy's jealous nature. She was used to winning, to pushing herself physically and mentally to take the prize at the end, knowing what to do to shave off a few seconds here and there to get the better time. But at the bank, it was really more of a chance of partiality, one she'd definitely lost.

Still squeezing the stress ball, she looked up as the bell above the door gave a jingle. A man walked in, his tall frame and expensive coat drawing her gaze. It was rare to find a good-looking guy who was taller than her but also a decent human being. Trace had failed at that last part after she'd needed a change in life, and he was determined not to let her forget it.

Her gaze traveled over the man's strong jawline, noting a slight stubble there. But it was the turquoise color of his eyes that drew her attention. Maybe it was the fact that she didn't recognize him that made him more attractive. The only unmarried men in this town weren't grown-up enough to care about a future. Her eyes flicked to his left hand. No ring.

"I can help you here," she said, forcing a smile on her face and breaking her gaze away.

Why did she check him out like that? She wasn't hunting for marriage at the moment. Her life was too undecided and all over the place. But then again, her best friend, Lauren, had married Walker, her older brother. Ever since then, she'd been wishing there was someone else she could connect with enough to go do things together.

The man who walked up to the desk seemed more familiar now that he was closer. Not in the went-to-high-school-with-him kind of way, which was possible in the small town of Coldwater Creek. He was either just passing through or here for a quick business trip because the suit of choice in Coldwater Creek was a pair of blue jeans and a flannel button-up.

He opened his coat to pull out a pen, revealing a well-tailored navy-blue suit, and the watch he sported had to cost more than she made in a year as a teller. That was about the only thing she'd learned while in the big city: which name brands cost how much.

PUSHING THOSE THOUGHTS AWAY, she focused on the check he handed her.

"I need to deposit this check into the account on the back," was all he said. It took a moment for her to register that he'd written the account number just under the signature on the back instead of filling out a deposit slip.

She nodded and said, "I can do that for you." The half-smile he gave her triggered a memory from years ago, a guy her brother's age who she'd had a crush on in the eighth grade. Dustin Wakefield.

She glanced away and stared at the name on the check, *B&G Family Investments, LLC,* she schooled her face when she saw the amount written on the bottom of it. Five hundred thousand dollars. She'd never seen a number that high in her years working there, but there was a first for everything.

"I just need to get my manager to sign off on this amount, and I'll get that taken care of for you."

Turning in her chair, Kassidy glanced over at him, his turquoise gaze causing her insides to flip. At the same time, her chunky heel caught on the metal rod at the bottom of the seat. Her hands kept her from face planting into her desk. She flushed and hurried over to the door to the manager's office without a backward glance. No need to see what a klutz she was written all over his face.

She knocked and opened the door then shut it behind her, facing her boss.

"What is it, Kassidy?" he asked, not looking up from his paperwork. The fact that he just assumed it was her caused bile to rise in her throat. He just needed to accept the fact that she was over his dramatics and move on.

"I have this—"

"I didn't promote you to loan officer because you have too many customer complaints, Kassidy. How are we supposed to give you more responsibility when people don't want to work with you anyway?" Trace glanced up, a hint of a smile on his face.

Nothing like a snarky comment to slice right through her.

"I actually came in to ask about signing off on this check, but it's good to know where you stand on my place at this bank." Her mind whirred with all her thoughts converging into one. "If there are no possibilities for me to progress in this company, then I'm done. Consider this my two-week notice."

She slapped the check down, allowing him to sign it.

He didn't even flinch when he saw the amount on the check. "Don't worry about two weeks. I'll get your final check ready now." No emotion, nothing that said he was sorry to see her go. If anything, that spurred her on even more. What a jerk! The fact that she'd ever had feelings for this guy made her skin crawl.

"If you're still harboring anger because I broke up with you last Christmas, why wait until now to talk about it?" Kassidy folded her arms across her chest, waiting for his response.

He shrugged. "You left. And now you're leaving the bank." Giving her a fake smile, he said, "We wish you well on your future endeavors." The smile dropped, and he glanced back down at the phone, dialing. When Rebecca picked up, he said, "I'm going to need a final check for Kassidy. She just quit." Trace gave her a quick hand wave out of the office.

Grabbing the check from his desk, Kassidy dropped it in front of Elaine and said, "Looks like you'll be helping this customer." She made sure to say it loud enough that the man heard. His eyes were curious before taking the two steps to the left.

Kassidy stormed into the back room and grabbed an empty box. Normally, she might have cared who was witnessing this scene, but with all that had happened today, adding a little flair to her exit wouldn't be the worst thing.

Once back at her desk, she started throwing her little trinkets into the box. She pulled the pictures off the short wall separating the fake cubicles where the tellers sat, placing them on top so they wouldn't be damaged.

Trace still hadn't come out with a check, so she sat in her chair, deleting off anything personal and logging out of her accounts on the computer.

"Tough day?" a deep voice asked, turning her attention to Dustin. The rich timbre of his voice confirmed that it was the heir to the Wakefield Mansion. Her fourteen-year-old self would have been doing flips that he was actually talking to her. Her twenty-five-year-old self was doing everything she could to keep her emotions from falling apart.

"Tough year," she said dryly. The more she thought about it, the more it rang true. She'd stopped racing after the NFR last year and had been so excited for Walker and Lauren and Easton and Natalie to settle into their lives as married couples. She'd thought her chance for that would come soon enough, like she was next in line. But it seemed she just kept getting passed up time and time again, in love and in her career.

"Don't worry. It's not the end of the road." Dustin flashed

her that half-smile again as a small measure of comfort warmed her.

Elaine finished up his transaction, and Kassidy saw him glance back at her before walking out the doors. Was that pity in his eyes? She didn't need pity, just applause at finally realizing the dead end her life had come to.

How had she let herself think that working at a bank was what she'd always wanted to do? A sense of relief that she was finally done there began mixing with the panic of how she would make money. There were only so many jobs in Coldwater Creek, and while she knew just about everything about horses and the rodeo, not many people offered to pay for that kind of stuff.

Her mind turned to the party she'd planned for Natalie's baby shower tomorrow. Party planning would be the ultimate dream come true, but who would be willing to pay for them and how far in between would the work be? Patty McCall had retired from event planning last year because she claimed there wasn't enough work to sustain her. She'd taken a job at the Wakefield Fabrication plant just up the road and looked like she was enjoying life more than when she ran her own business.

"Here is your final check. Thank you for the years you've been with us, and I wish you good luck." Trace's voice sounded like a robot, and Kassidy had heard those words before, said to the last loan officer who'd left for another branch.

"Why are you acting like I'm leaving town?" she said, lifting her box and walking to the door. "It's a small town. It's not like we're never going to see each other again."

She stormed out of there, finally able to breathe again. She'd have to take her final check and the rest of her money to the other bank in town. Setting foot into this one to make transactions would only score her pity or arrogance, and she didn't need either.

Loading the box into her old Jeep, she glanced at the peeling paint and the numerous rock chips in the windshield. It would be a while before she'd be able to upgrade now. Where was she going, and why wasn't there some big billboard to signal what she was supposed to do with her life?

*N*othing like an unexpected show in a small town.

Dustin Wakefield had fired a fair number of people, even watched a few of them go on their own terms, but something about the scene he'd just witnessed made him laugh, like it was straight out of a comedy. The woman who'd helped him initially looked like she was ready for war by the time Dustin had walked out of the bank.

Now, glancing to his right, he saw her throwing her stuff into an old beat-up Jeep. He studied her features, surprised at how attractive she looked while she stomped around the vehicle brushing the thin blanket of snow from the windows.

He should probably get out and help her. That's the kind of person his grandmother had raised. But the warmth coming from the heater was thawing out the chill in his bones. He'd thought he wouldn't have a problem coming back to this small valley after all these years. It took a minute for him to count how long it had been since he'd been here. Two years since his grandfather's funeral. But he'd practically just flown into the airport in Jackson that time and then taken off again the next morning. The last time he'd really seen the valley was when he'd packed everything he could fit into his SUV and driven to LA eight years ago.

After another minute of hesitation where he sat rooted to the driver's seat, he watched as the woman opened her door and got in, her cheeks bright pink from the cold. She turned in his direction, and her eyes widened like she was horrified he was still there. As she pulled out of the parking lot, he chastised himself for being so selfish.

And then he brushed it off. He'd be here for a grand total of four weeks, which was longer than he wanted to be back. But his grandmother had called, wanting him to come and throw the Christmas Gala at the Wakefield Mansion on Christmas Eve. And spend Christmas with her, just like old times, she'd said. There was only so much negotiating he could do when it came to Grace Wakefield, the woman who'd raised him.

As much as he'd tried to debate his need to stay in the city and work from the offices, as long as there was an internet connection, he could conduct business as the CEO for Wakefield Fabrication from anywhere around the world. He'd finally relented, and twenty-four hours later, he'd begun the thirteen-plus-hour drive to Coldwater Creek.

As he stared out at the snowflakes falling from the sky now, he couldn't help but long for the scenery from the last few Christmases. Beaches, sun, the opportunity to travel.

He pulled out onto the main road, memories popping up from his childhood here. Pushing them away, he didn't want to live in the past. He wanted to move on and keep going forward. His brain called up a mental image of the bank teller, and he smiled, wondering which of the handful of families who settled the valley she belonged to, or if she'd moved in since he'd left.

He was the owner of a Fortune 500 company, and all the women who usually gave him attention were only after one thing, maybe two: his money and a diamond ring on the right finger. It was tempting to pretend he was someone else, to give people in town a false name to avoid the kind of attention he usually garnered when he was introduced. But something always kept him from doing that. Probably his inability to keep a straight face when he lied.

Taking the turn that led up to the hill where the mansion sat, he put everything about the teller out of his mind. He had a job to do while he was here. Not one he particularly wanted to do, but one that had to be done to make the best decisions for the company as a whole.

The phone rang, his grandmother's picture popping up on the screen. He pressed the connect button on the steering wheel and said, "Hello, Grandmother."

"Dusty, it's so good to hear your voice. Did you already leave LA? You forgot to call and tell me if you left. I always worry you'll be in an accident or something." For an eighty-five-year-old woman, she still knew how to lay on the guilt.

He glanced at the clock on the dashboard and grinned. "I'm almost to the mansion, Grandma," he said, waiting for her response.

She gasped. "What time did you leave this morning? It's only noon."

"I stayed over in St. George last night. I had to meet with the factory managers there, and then I got up early this morning to get on the road." More like he'd barely slept. Major changes were coming to the company, and he'd been sorting through information for the past three months to figure out how best to incorporate them at each of the fifty-one factories around the nation. He'd gone to sleep closer to two in the morning and then was up around five. That's what insomnia and a good measure of stress had done to his sleeping since he'd taken control of the company four years ago. "At least I missed the big storm moving through Northern Utah on my way."

"I'm sure it will end up coming through anyway, but I'm glad you're safe. I've had Margritte make up your old room for you. I wish you could've come yesterday for Thanksgiving, but I just hope you'll stick around longer than Christmas." Sadness filled her voice, and the air in Dustin's chest caught. Christmas had always been an exciting time at the mansion, and he knew she was hoping to recreate it after the loss of Grandpa two years before.

He crested the hill and was surprised by the sight of the house. It was still in pristine condition, the outside of it looking like it had just been built. He pressed the garage door opener he'd kept in a drawer at home for so long it had become dusty.

Taking a deep breath, he shifted into park and nodded. "We'll see how things go, Grandma. There's a lot of work, and Coldwater Creek isn't the easiest place to travel in and out of, especially during the winter." He glanced around, seeing that the grounds already boasted several inches of fresh white powder. He hadn't really thought of snow travel. His car might not make it through some of the roads if a big storm blew in while he was here.

She hung up the phone in her usual abrupt way. Saying goodbye had been too sentimental for her since Dustin's grandfather had passed away from old age.

"Dusty," his grandmother's voice called, only this time it was from the door connecting the garage to the rest of the mansion. "It's so good to have you home." She waited for him to climb the steps and wrapped him in a warm hug.

When he took a step back, he was surprised to see how thin and frail she'd become over the past few months. She'd come to visit him during the summer months in LA with Margritte, her personal maid and nurse.

"I don't know if this is really home anymore," he said, taking off his shoes next to the built-in shelving his grandfather had contracted out when Dustin had come to live with them. It had been the catch-all for just about everything, and the emptiness of the space felt strange, like he no longer existed there.

"It will always be your home, dear. And when I'm gone, you'll fill it with your family. Give your future children the kind of childhood you had." Her eyes moistened, and she clapped her hands together like she was praying for exactly that.

Dustin groaned, not wanting to go into this again with her. She'd been talking about her future great-grandchildren since Dustin graduated from college, but the betrayals he still felt from past relationships had erected into a solid concrete barrier, not letting any woman affect him more than he had to deal with her.

Just as he thought that, the girl from the bank came to mind, and he gave a quick smile. "It will be better in the hands of someone who already has a family, Grandma. Not for some workaholic bachelor."

"I'm glad you mentioned that," she said, slipping her hand into the crook of his arm and pointing for them to head to the family room of the house. She took a seat in a recliner, her breathing more labored than Dustin was used to. The signs of age were written around her eyes, and the way her back bent just a little more pierced him. "You need to hire some people, train them well. Give them tasks that you don't need to be doing anymore and just deal with the bigger stuff."

Dustin took a seat in the matching recliner on the other side of the sofa, rocking back and forth a minute before he smiled at her. "Grandfather never hired anyone to do stuff like that."

Her reaction was what he'd expected. Her lips pursed, and

her eyebrows cinched together in frustration. She'd worn that expression plenty of times throughout his teen years when he'd said or done something she didn't approve of.

"I don't care what your grandfather did or didn't do. When the factories were down for the day, so was he, here reading a book. Now, with all the technology, the work never stops." She leaned forward a bit, resting her hands on her knees. "You're almost thirty, Dusty. What are you going to do with the money you're earning anyway? Put it in your bank account and never spend it?"

Her remark caused bitterness to rise in his throat. She and his grandfather had built the Wakefield Empire by being frugal and making the right deals at the right time. Shouldn't he do the same?

"I just don't want to fail this company. I don't want to fail Grandpa's legacy." The words burned with the truth. There was always the fear of failure there, lurking around the corners of his mind. He hated defeat, and the few times he'd taken a risk and then failed had burned holes into his memory, making him remember every vivid detail to the point that he didn't want to relive that again.

Her expression softened, and even though his mother had only married into the Wakefield family, the similarities between her and Grandmother had been vast. That look was one he remembered, even after he'd forgotten most of the other things that had tied him to his deceased parents.

"You're not going to fail. From what I've heard, things are going well." She sat back, accepting a cup of tea from Margritte.

"Can I get you anything, Dustin?" the woman asked.

"No, thank you, Margritte." He smiled and then added, "Thank you for taking such good care of my grandmother."

The heavyset woman grinned and waved a hand through the air. "I think you're mistaken, sir. She's the one always taking care of me." She turned and walked back into the kitchen, and Dustin could feel his grandmother's eyes on him again. He needed to explain the most recent changes he'd be making to the company, but the thought of her reaction caused him to pause before doing so.

"I might have to shut down the plant here in Coldwater Creek." The words were out, and a measure of relief settled over him. He'd been trying to figure out how to tell her for the past few weeks, ever since the big numbers had come in from the third quarter. Production was down almost double compared to the other facilities, and unless he could find some miracle that would cure that, they'd have to close the plant and move the rest of the operations to the one in Colorado.

"There have been rumors of that floating around town as well, from what Margritte tells me." Her voice was soft, each word deliberate. "Is it really that bad?"

"I'll know more once I meet with the managers this week. I just hope to be able to save the decision for after the new year."

His grandmother nodded. "Just make sure to look at all the options before you close. This valley relies a lot on the plant, and I would hate to see the town die because of it." She took another sip of tea, then her features brightened. "I need your help with something. Our usual planner for the Christmas Gala is unavailable this year."

Dustin raised an eyebrow. "Please don't ask me to fill in for that." He chuckled, and she swatted the air with a sigh.

"Of course not! But I need your help finding a new planner. Preferably someone local so he or she can make sure to get all the details right and in order before the big night."

"I know nothing about event planners, Grandma. I can always ask Sandra back in the office to find someone." He closed his eyes a moment, enjoying the feeling of not being in a car anymore.

His grandmother waved her hand and shook her head. "No, this won't take long. Can't you post an ad to the local paper or on some of those social media platforms? And then I'll need your help choosing one of them."

"I have so much to do already, Grandma. Can't Margritte help you with it?" Dustin leaned his head back against the recliner, staring at the chandelier hanging from the vaulted ceiling.

"I won't be around forever, Dusty. You used to love watching the house come to life with Christmas decorations. I think this would be a fun activity for both of us and would only take a couple of hours in the next few days to accomplish. You could use a set break in your workload and give me the opportunity to find out how you're really doing." She smiled, oozing guilt into him.

"Fine. I'll help when I can. But no major promises."

She drained the rest of her cup of tea and set it back on the table next to her. "Dusty, I think you can use a nap. Those always help me when I'm feeling overwhelmed."

Laughing, Dustin said, "I never said I was overwhelmed."

"You didn't have to. Your face tells me everything I need to know." She grinned and stared at him for a bit. She'd always been able to read him like a book.

"I'll work on that this week. We've still got a few weeks until the gala." He stood, knowing he needed to unpack his car and get settled. It was the afternoon of Black Friday, but he still had a lot of work ahead of him for the weekend.

"We have less than four weeks until the gala, Dusty. Time is going to go fast if you don't have someone hired in the next week."

"I'll put it on my to-do list," he said, not excited to be in charge of finding a person to plan the party. He spent enough time interviewing people for positions in the business aspect of the company or making sure they were all trained to manage the various factories throughout the states. Interviewing party planners was low on his list of things to get accomplished before the new year.

He had a lot of people underneath him who could give him an answer within a few minutes for who would be best to organize the traditional gala. But even he would admit his grandmother was right. She didn't have much time left, and if this was one of the things she'd wanted him to come home for, he'd find the time to do it.

CHAPTER 3

Kassidy did her best to smile and laugh, pushing off the panic of no longer being employed that threatened to undo her. No, she'd never liked her job at the bank, but being unemployed in a town as small as Coldwater Creek meant she might have to live with her parents forever. The thought made her want to cry.

Okay, that was a bit dramatic, but her brain was making it hard to be positive right now. The one thing that distracted her was getting things ready for the baby shower her sister-in-law, Natalie, had asked her to throw.

She and Easton had gotten married after only being engaged for two months, and a few weeks after the honeymoon, they'd revealed she was already expecting. Kassidy's twin brothers would not let it go that Natalie and Easton were having a honeymoon baby. But their mother was ecstatic to finally become a grandma.

Natalie had asked Kassidy to plan the baby shower three months ago, allowing her free rein with theme and decorations. It had been the thing Kassidy looked forward to every day after work, checking her ClipBoard app to get ideas for the perfect party.

She'd gone with a woodland theme since the couple had decided not to find out whether they were having a boy or a girl. That in itself irked Kassidy. How were people supposed to know what gifts to bring for the shower if nobody knew what they were having?

Neutral was her best bet, and she'd spent much of the night before frosting the cupcakes to look like red-topped mushrooms and sewing together the rest of the bunting that hung between the two large trees out back. She wouldn't have been able to sleep much anyway. The replay of the scene at the bank kept cycling through her brain, making it hard to focus on anything else.

It was the perfect fall day for a shower, and Kassidy hoped the snow would stay at bay for another couple of weeks. The holiday weekend had made it impossible for some of the guests to make it, but it was the only time Natalie's mother could come from Utah. Overall, it was a decent turnout for the favorite English teacher at Coldwater Creek High.

Arms wrapped around her shoulders, and Kassidy turned to see Natalie smiling at her.

"You are amazing at this," she said, motioning to the decorations. "Maybe this is your calling." She winked at Kassidy, waddling away to talk to some woman calling her over.

For a split second, Kassidy contemplated that thought again. And then she shook it off. There was no way she could make a living doing this for the small town. If Patty had tried to do it her whole life and finally retired early at fifty-five last year, unable to make it, how could she? Then again, no one had really been a fan of Patty's ideas and visions.

Once the presents had all been opened, a bunch of the ladies sat around chatting. Kassidy took a seat next to her mother and aunt, taking a sip of the lemonade and finally eating one of the mini sandwiches she'd made early that morning.

"You've done an outstanding job with this, Kass," Aunt Wendy said, grinning at her. "Much better than any I've ever been to. Did you learn all this when you were in the city?"

Kassidy tried not to laugh. The members of her family who'd lived in the valley since birth always looked at those who went away to the city as the smartest and most talented people in the world. Being there for about four months wasn't enough time to learn much of anything.

"Come on, Wendy," Kassidy's mom said, slapping her sister lightly on the leg. "She's always been like this. Do you remember when Taylor had a painting birthday? Kassidy missed out on the rest of the activities because she was trying to finish her creation."

Kassidy smiled shyly at the thought. It had been a long time since her cousin's birthday party, but the small canvas she'd painted that day still hung in her bedroom.

"I think you should at least look into it," Aunt Wendy said, swiping crumbs off the front of her blouse. "This valley could use someone good in the party-planning department. Do you remember Uncle Alan's sixtieth birthday party? Someone bought a giant cake and a couple of streamers and called it good."

The three of them laughed at that, and Kassidy chuckled at the thought.

"Thanks, you two. This is a fun hobby, for sure. I just need to find something else to do in the meantime. Now that I'm not at the bank, I mean."

Aunt Wendy leaned forward. "Not the most creative thing, but Wakefield Fabrication is hiring."

That was definitely a creativity crusher. Standing in lines and pushing parts through the machinery was the last thing she wanted to do. But it might be something she had to do just to stay out of debt. Her parents wouldn't save her from using hard work to get to where she needed to go, and it was nice to have a plan to fall back on.

"How are things down there?" my mom asked her sister. Aunt Wendy had worked on the lines for the past thirty years. She'd been promoted to line supervisor recently, which was more than Kassidy had done at the bank.

"It's going all right. Production is down, and there have been rumors that the corporate office is going to close us down." It had been a while since Aunt Wendy was serious about anything, but not even a hint of a smile crossed her face.

Kassidy gasped. "Closing down the factory would mean most of the town would be out of work, wouldn't it?"

Aunt Wendy nodded, frustration ebbing across her features.

Kassidy's parents had spoken about the importance of the factory to the valley from time to time, saying that the town would practically die if the factory ever shut down. There weren't enough jobs within commuting distance to make it worth sticking around.

"What's changed that makes them want to shut things down?" Kassidy asked.

Aunt Wendy shrugged. "I'm not sure, to be honest. I just overheard Darrell saying the CEO of the company was going to be meeting with all the managers and supervisors next week."

That's why Dustin Wakefield had come back to town.

There was only one family in town with the billion-dollar status to dress the way that man did and even to drive the type of car he drove. No one in their right mind would drive a Maserati this close to winter in Coldwater Creek.

She focused on the mental picture of his face, his

turquoise eyes and the strong cut of his jaw. Even after several years, he'd only aged for the better. Not like she had a chance there. He'd been witness to her leaving the bank.

"They're probably meeting with Dustin Wakefield, then," Kassidy said slowly, focusing on pulling a piece of the sandwich apart so she didn't see their reactions. Many a notebook had been signed with Kassidy Wakefield in the wishing of a teenage girl that an attractive older guy would notice her. And it seemed like no one would let her forget it.

"You saw him?" Kassidy's mother asked, that knowing smile crossing her face.

"He came into the bank yesterday. He was the customer I was helping when I quit." She raised her finger to her lips. "I know what you're going to say, and I think you should just… not say it. He was just a teenage crush, and we're not even on the same playing field now."

Her mother and Aunt Wendy giggled, trying to hide it behind sips of punch. Kassidy rolled her eyes, wondering how it was possible to grow up but still be sent back to her fifteen-year-old self with the mention of one guy's name.

"I just hope the rumors aren't a sure thing. But Dustin coming back to the valley is probably more of a sign of the apocalypse than anything, I'd wager," Aunt Wendy said when they'd composed themselves.

Kassidy's interest perked up. "Why is that?"

"I overheard his grandfather when he came to the factory a few years ago—before he died, of course—say that when Dustin came to Coldwater Creek again, it would be either a miracle or a sign that things were ending."

Some kind of prophecy? They weren't in a magical world by any means. What had happened to the Wakefield heir that made him not want to come to their small town?

There were definitely more exciting places to be, and LA had plenty to entertain, if that was where he still lived. She'd seen articles about him from time to time, but she'd realized that dating him had a slim-to-none chance of happening after she'd seen him posing with a different woman at each event he went to, all refined and looking like runway models.

Kassidy was well acquainted with the beauty queens who rode horses and competed in rodeos. She was to those girls what Coldwater Creek was to LA, where the two-screen movie theater took an extra two months compared to the rest of the world to get the latest movies playing in it.

She couldn't worry about that now. She needed goals, something to aim for that was actually achievable.

A hand rested on her shoulder, and she glanced up, seeing Natalie's mother smiling at her.

"Kassidy, you've done an amazing job with the party. Thank you for doing this for Natalie." She reached out her arms, and Kassidy stood, stepping into the hug.

"It was a pleasure to plan it for her."

"We've been trying to convince Kassidy that she needs to start a party-planning business," Aunt Wendy said, her sly smile causing Kassidy to laugh.

Natalie's mom nodded. "I think that would be a great idea. We have events with my husband's work all the time, and you'd be worth the hire after some of the disasters from years past. I'll let him know for the next one."

The party wrapped up, and as Kassidy sent off the last of the mini treats with some of the guests, she couldn't get Dustin's words from the day before out of her mind, that it wasn't the end of the road. She wondered if that been some sort of insight into what he was doing here in the valley. That he was about to let all these people go and just tell them it wasn't the end of the road.

Now the words that had comforted her less than twenty-four hours ago burned in her throat as she closed one of the fold-up chairs with more force than she thought, causing a loud bang.

Eyes turned in her direction, and she forced a smile and kept going, knowing she wouldn't have to deal with him again anytime soon. And if by chance she did see him, she'd give him a piece of her mind.

As much as there were times when she thought their town was too little, that everyone knew her business before she did, there was so much to love about the people. And the thought of it withering away to the few ranchers who lived in the valley would make it a lonely existence. Not to mention she'd eventually have to leave to find work, and at the moment, she'd had enough of the city.

Several ladies, relatives or citizens of the community, walked by and complimented her on how beautiful the shower had been. One asked if she'd thought about doing something for weddings. It was a temptation to go full-on with this, but she gave a tentative yes. With enough time to plan things, she might be able to pull something off.

But what if she failed?

That was the overarching question of all of it. She'd never failed at something so big as a life-changing decision like her career. Falling off a horse during the middle of a race was a failure, but this felt ten times as hard as that, like her entire ego was at stake.

But if that's the only way she was going to move on, she would have to put her head down and work through it. She'd been through tough situations, and as hard as they'd been at the time, she'd managed to make it through them. Whether she was supposed to be an event planner or a girl on the line at the fabrication plant, she'd have to just take things one day at a time in the hopes that she'd figure it out.

CHAPTER 4

The sign in the diner window said closed, and Dustin's stomach growled in protest. He'd forgotten that most stores closed early in Coldwater Creek, especially on a Saturday night. He'd meant to get into town earlier, had planned to get several things checked off his to-do list, but he'd gotten held up on a call from a client back east. His grandmother had then asked him to join her for lunch. After that, it seemed like a time warp had sucked the day away.

At least the grocery store was still open. He'd already gone through the cupboards and pantry, cringing as he saw all the healthy stuff, including fiber and prune juice well-stocked. Sure, he was twenty-nine, but that didn't always mean he ate like a responsible adult. Sugared cereal and microwaveable entrees were what he kept in his cupboards for when he was sick of takeout and dinner meetings.

It had been a long time since he'd actually made time to cook a full meal, usually grabbing something between calls and emails. Margritte did well enough making the food for his grandmother's meals, but he was going to have to stop at the fast-food restaurant on the way back home. The gluten-free bread and stale chips just didn't satisfy.

With a shopping cart loaded with bread, peanut butter, chips, and cookies, as well as the handheld frozen pizzas he craved, he turned down the aisle, looking for dry pasta.

A message pinged, a quick echo of the tone bouncing off the shelves. He pulled out his phone, still steering the cart around the corner. His eyes were on the phone for so long that he didn't see anyone through his periphery.

The cart smacked into something, and he jerked his head up, trying to figure out what it was. He was relieved to see it wasn't one of those large displays of goods tumbling to the ground. But as he stepped to the side of his cart to see what he'd bumped into, a familiar face glance up. She was bent over holding her ankle. The teller from the bank.

He walked around the cart and reached out a hand to her. "I'm sorry about that. I—" He broke off, gesturing to the phone in his hand.

"There's a reason why they say not to text and drive. Maybe you should heed that advice," she said, scowling at him. She avoided his hand and stood up on her own, brushing her hands together. She must have discovered who he was. He wasn't used to a reaction that harsh, but the people of Coldwater Creek could be very protective.

Dustin allowed his lips to turn up just a bit. "True. When it's something for work, I sometimes get tunnel vision." He paused, not knowing what else to say. He ran a national company, and it wasn't often that he didn't have the right phrase on the tip of his tongue.

"A little time off never hurt anyone," she said, picking up the small basket she'd set on the floor.

Before Dustin could stop himself, he said, "How's that working out for you?" He bit his upper lip, trying to curb the emotional rollercoaster she'd set him on. One minute he was attracted to her, and then next, she was spewing venom all over him.

She glared at him, her jaw twitching a few times before she stepped toward the shelves. "I'll give you plenty of room before you run into me again."

Dustin chuckled and took that as his cue to leave. He gave a curt nod and continued on, grabbing a couple of boxes of pasta and pasta sauce. With a quick glance back before he turned out of the aisle, he saw the woman turn her head quickly to focus on the products in front of her. He'd caught her watching him walk away. That shouldn't even interest him, but there was something about her that made him want to know more.

No. He didn't have time for that. He'd be heading back to California after Christmas anyway. No time to get tangled up to leave again anyway. And his luck with women in this town was abysmal. Okay, so there had just been the one betrayal in the valley, while the other two were from California. That just solidified that the two places he'd lived in his life were blacklisted as locations to find someone he could have a lasting relationship with.

He scooted the cart up next to the register and waited in front of the credit card reader, watching as the cashier checked the items through.

"Did you find everything you needed?" the young girl asked, swiping things with almost a second instinct about where the bar codes were. Dustin had tried the self-checkouts back in LA, and he was sure it had taken him almost twice the amount of time as a seasoned professional.

"I did, thank you." He paused a moment. This girl looked to be about seventeen, eighteen. Maybe she had an idea of someone he could contact about a party planner.

"Is there some kind of event coordinator or business here in town?"

The girl chewed her gum a couple of times and kept sliding things over the scanner. She shrugged. "My parents won't let me plan parties. The one old lady who used to do it retired last year. Although if you ask me, that lady was destined for fifty cats and a bookshelf full of romance novels."

Dustin tried to smile, not sure why the girl had given that much of an explanation. He wasn't sure how to react to that one.

"If she's got the room for them, cats can be quite the company." He pulled out his card and handed it to her.

She scanned a few other items before she said, "Kassidy might be able to plan one, though. She did a great job at a baby shower I went to today."

"Kassidy who?" Dustin asked, wondering if he could check another thing off his list tonight. Having an event planner lined up would also keep his grandmother happy and let him get back to the real reason he'd come to the valley.

"McBride. She lives on one of the ranches past the creek."

By the time the girl had finished the transaction, Dustin was just ready to be in his car. He wouldn't have to talk to any other strangers for the rest of the night, besides whoever took his order at the drive-thru. He could interact with people well enough, but sometimes he just needed a break in between to recharge.

Was a seventeen-year-old a good source for an event planner? The connection from baby shower to planning the annual gala was quite a jump in expertise and style.

After loading things into his sports car, Dustin turned around and saw the woman he'd hit down the pasta aisle. She glanced up at him and then focused on the keys in her hand.

"Sorry again about hitting you. I hope your leg is okay."

"Thank you," she said. Then she hesitated, curiosity

spreading over her features. "Why did you say that quitting the bank wasn't the end of the road?"

Dustin took a step back, trying to remember why he'd said that. "Um, just trying to help you feel like life wasn't over? I don't know."

"You weren't trying to allude to why you're here in town after a decade?" she asked, her hands emphasizing her words.

"Eight years," he said defensively. "And I'm not sure who you are more than Kassidy from your name tag."

Her eyes widened, and her nose flared. She turned on her heel and hurried into her car. Winning friends, it seemed, here in Coldwater Creek.

Not that he was biting on that kind of bait, but there hadn't been many times a girl or woman had turned him down, or didn't try to throw themselves at him. That had to be the only reason he was curious about her. She didn't put on airs or try to seem like she was better than most. She just avoided him. And yelled at him, but he *had* run into her with his cart. It was…refreshing.

By the time he arrived back at the house, the sun had begun to set, and the long list he'd meant to accomplish was left unchecked. At least his grandma wasn't home to harass him about it.

After a quick internet search, he found nothing about event planners within fifty miles around the town. He didn't even bother to search the name of the girl the cashier had given him. The job would go to a professional so he wouldn't have to worry about the details of the party all month long. Hiring someone to do all that was a good use of money, saving him time to focus on the affairs of the business.

While he put away some of the items he'd bought, he noticed a list of numbers taped to the inside of the cupboard next to where the landline used to sit.

Dora Seeley was the first name on the list and one of his

grandmother's best friends. She'd always been the town gossip, finding out information about him before he even knew. If the woman was still alive and her number was still in service, she might be the one to ask about a planner. Then he could tell his grandmother he was at least making progress on what was supposed to be their joint venture.

The phone rang several times, an encouraging sound since he'd been sure it was disconnected. The landline to the mansion had been turned off a few years ago after Dustin had taught his grandmother how to use a cell phone.

"Hello?" came a frail voice on the other end.

"Hi, is this the number to find Dora Seeley?"

"It is."

Dustin paused for a few seconds, waiting for her to say she was the woman he was looking for. When she didn't say anything, he said, "This is Grace Wakefield's grandson. I'm just calling—"

"Dusty? What a pleasure it is to get a call from you. I've seen a few articles about your accomplishments, and I cut them out and saved them. You can come by and see."

"I will have to do that," Dustin submitted, not sure he'd be able to find the time. "Ms. Seeley, I was wondering if you know of anyone who can plan events here in the valley? I'm trying to get the gala going for this year—"

"Oh, dear. Don't you think you're a little late to be starting that? Your grandmother always has someone ready to start with plans by October 1st."

Guilt and worry sliced through him. Not deep enough to do permanent damage, but enough to make it sting. He'd never paid attention to when things got started, just that after Thanksgiving, the house was slowly and thoroughly transformed into a Christmas dream. Well, his dream every year had been to turn back time and that his parents wouldn't have taken that flight in a snowstorm just to see his class play. His nine-year-old self had whined that they wouldn't make it, and it was his fault they were dead.

Brushing off the memories and swallowing down the knot in his throat, he said, "Grandma just asked me to help her find someone. Apparently, the last one quit the business or couldn't do it this year."

"I haven't heard of any new planners, but you might want to post it on the town group page. I'm sure someone will want to apply for the position."

Why hadn't he thought of that? Maybe because he wanted to be told right then a name and number of a person qualified to take on such a big job. Like his grandmother said, there were only a few weeks until Christmas, and he needed to hire someone as soon as possible. But an application process might be a good idea to get the best planner for the job.

Once he ended the call, he searched for the town social page on the internet and created an account in order to post. At least they weren't so far behind the times like he'd always thought growing up.

Submitting his query, he wondered if he'd even get any offers.

CHAPTER 5

Guys were jerks. Especially ones who wore expensive suits, even to the grocery store. Kassidy hadn't been in sweats, but she'd definitely relaxed after a long day of bridal shower setup and takedown.

Of all the people to run into her, it had to be Dustin Wakefield. And then he'd asked the cashier who she was. How she'd ever had a crush on him was beyond her. The guy obviously didn't care about anyone but himself or he wouldn't even think about shutting down the factory. Here she was, two days later, still having make-believe conversations with him in her head. If only she could be that direct and consistent in real life.

She rubbed at her eyes, trying to wake up enough to get dressed and head downstairs. This Monday was worse than when she had to get up for work at the bank, which surprised her. Probably because Kassidy didn't have an idea of what to do with herself and her future.

As she headed out to help Easton with the morning chores, the smell of a coming storm swirled in the air. They'd been lucky not to have several storms already, and part of her was excited for all things winter. On the other hand, she'd have cabin fever by January, so she needed to come up with something to do with her time. A job would be nice.

She'd always loved the ranch, but this was Easton's territory now. Their father had turned it over to him several months ago after a doctor's visit found some small tumors. Easton and Natalie were almost done building a house on the property next to their parents, and Kassidy was glad the place would be taken care of no matter where she ended up.

"Why do you look like the weight of the world is on your shoulders, little sis?" Easton asked, pulling up in his truck. He'd been out in the back fields mending a fence that some of the cows had snuck through. That was the story of his life.

Kassidy shook her head. "Just trying to figure out my future, and it's not going well." She stabbed the pitchfork into another clump of hay, moving it over for the animals. "I feel like I failed."

Easton's deep chuckle made her smile against her will. He'd always been quick to laugh, except for when things hadn't been going well between him and Natalie when they started dating last year. Kassidy heard bits and pieces of the story when Easton explained it to their mother, but she did know he'd faced his fair share of obstacles over the years.

"Then you're probably on the right track to figuring out what you want."

"Awesome. You're telling me I know what I want to do with my life while I have no clue? I mean, I went to the city and made it all of four months before I came home. I got passed over for a promotion, but there's a lot that went into that situation. And I'll probably be living in Mom and Dad's house forever."

Easton's easy-going smile dropped. "When you say it like that, it's kind of a self-fulfilling prophecy. What would make you happy?"

Kassidy stopped to think about that, wiping a bead of sweat from her forehead despite the temperature. Moving hay was a tough job no matter the weather.

"Can you really have a job that makes you happy? Isn't it all just suffering through the days to get a paycheck and then occasionally going on trips to see other places?" she chuckled, but her words didn't sit well.

"If you look at it like that, you'll never be happy."

Kassidy sighed. "I know. I wish there was some neon sign that pointed in the direction I need to go."

"It took me a bit to see that I wanted to be a rancher. I love Dad, but sometimes I just wanted to try something else, felt like I needed to get away to understand what I wanted. Ever since he let me take over, I'm the happiest I've ever been, even though I couldn't coach football this fall. Well, Natalie has had a good part in that too." He grinned, his eyes drifting off to the house.

Jealousy and disappointment seared through Kassidy's chest, and she knew she needed to get back to work to push away the thoughts of loneliness.

She wasn't dumb and didn't think that finding a man would solve all of her problems. In fact, it was probably a blessing that she hadn't found someone yet, just so she could get her head on straight.

"Don't give up, Kass," Easton said, his arm draped out the window and tapping the side of the truck. "You'll figure it out soon enough. Just get rid of those negative thoughts, will ya?"

Kassidy frowned at him before he drove off to another part of the property.

She finished up the chores around the outside of the house, taking in the beauty of the softly falling flakes. Grabbing some firewood, she brought it in and set it next to the wood stove in the corner of the main room. The weather hadn't dropped down to the frigid temperatures that usually came with the snow, but it was only a matter of hours at this point.

"Looks like you got up early this morning," her mother said with a wink. On the days she had to work at the bank, she usually slept in until the very last minute before she threw on her business attire and ran a brush through her hair.

"I figured I needed to earn my keep for the foreseeable future, until I decide what I'm going to do." She heard the bitterness in her tone, and Easton's words about being more positive floated through her mind. She'd definitely have to work on that.

"I think I've got an idea to help you figure that out." Her mom was practically dancing as she grinned at Kassidy.

"Am I going to hate this idea?" Kassidy asked, teasing.

"Of course not. When have my ideas been bad?" Her mother feigned hurt, and Kassidy laughed.

"That time you told me to go out with Bobby Turner and we ended up in a ditch for six hours until someone rescued us." Kassidy paused and then said, "When you didn't tell me not to date my high school boyfriend and now former boss, Trace."

Her mother pointed at her. "Touché. Yeah, that was not one of my better suggestions. But this one is; I promise."

Kassidy hadn't noticed the laptop on the counter in front of her mother, and when it was turned toward her, she saw the Coldwater Creek page pulled up.

"Mom, you know I'm horrible at spelling. Working for the town paper or the town announcement page is just a bad idea all around." Kassidy leaned both elbows on the counter, the exhaustion from the morning already wearing on her.

"No, that's not what this is about," her mother said, glancing back at the screen. "Oh, I thought I'd clicked on it."

She leaned in and clicked a box in the lower corner, allowing it to zoom in so it was readable.

"Wanted: Event Planner."

Kassidy paused, trying to figure out if she was excited about that idea or not. She really did love planning parties. Reading on, she saw that it was for the Christmas Gala on Christmas Eve at Wakefield Mansion.

"They don't have someone for it already? Mrs. Wakefield is usually on top of it before Halloween decorations appear. And why would they be having the gala if they're shutting down our plant? Isn't that like a slap in the face to our town?"

Her mother glared at her, shaking her head. "Kass, we don't know for sure that's what's going to happen. Maybe it was just time for him to come home. We don't know that closing the plant is on his agenda. And why are you all ornery about it?"

Kassidy leaned her hand on the counter with a sigh. As she thought over her mother's question, she thought about her aunt's words at the baby shower. She loved this little town, and to think of it going the way of a ghost town tugged at her chest, making it hard to breathe. She glanced back at the screen and read all the details. "The gala is three and a half weeks away."

"All you have to do is apply for it. If you don't get it, then you tried. But if you do, can you imagine decorating that place? That would be amazing." Her mother was starry-eyed, and Kassidy could understand why.

Wakefield Mansion was one of the coolest places when she was younger. She'd only been inside twice, and that was just because the grandmother had invited her in when she'd ventured up there to sell some kind of fundraiser to help pay for barrel racing. The place was massive, making her parents' spacious house look like a shoebox.

Kassidy reached over and clicked on the link in the box,

which took her to a form. She scrolled down without filling in anything, just to check and see if it was even worth it to start. Decorating the mansion would be surreal, if she even got to that part.

She scrolled through question after question, shocked that the form was nearly twenty-five questions long. And there was the kicker at the end: *How many years of experience do you have?*

"I'm not filling this out, Mom. If I get to interview for this, he'll know I have no experience."

"Why? You'll be perfect for this. I can't think of anyone in town who'd be better for the position." Her mother smiled at her, reaching over and tucking back a section of hair that had escaped Kassidy's messy ponytail from all the work and wind that morning.

"What am I going to put? 'Planned a baby shower for thirty people. Oh, and by the way, how did you like the way I stormed out at the bank after I quit?'" Kassidy dropped her face into her hands. Not to mention the way she'd treated him at the grocery store. "A place like Wakefield Mansion is going to need a whole crew of people to set up and get ready."

Her mother wrapped an arm around her shoulders and pulled her in, surrounding Kassidy with the smell of cinnamon and fresh bread.

"But you might as well apply. You never know. And then you can apply for a few more. Maybe even make a website and just get started."

Kassidy bit the inside of her cheek, looking at her mom with the most vulnerable look she'd ever let anyone see. "What if it fails, Mom?"

"Then we find something else. We never let you give up when you fell off the horse. This is one of those things. You try it until you're sure it's not working and then move on.

But I have a feeling you won't need to move on from this one."

Her mom patted her back. "I've got to run to the store to get some things for dinner. Let me know if you need anything."

Kassidy sat on a stool and brought the computer toward her. She'd never been this nervous about anything, and the level of self-doubt and excitement at the prospect caused her fingers to stop midair above the keyboard. Usually she had a little swagger and confidence, but that seemed to be hiding ever since she'd stood up to her boss at the bank.

Blowing out a breath, she set her fingers on the keys and started typing. What did she have to lose?

CHAPTER 6

here did all these people come from?

Dustin checked the number of responses he'd gotten around midday on Monday. Forty-six applications.

No one had been able to point him in the direction of a real event planner since he'd arrived a few days ago. And now forty-six people were claiming to know enough to decorate a mansion?

He took a shower, trying to figure out how to narrow that number down faster than interviewing each one. He didn't have a ton of experience in the actual organization of events, but he'd been to enough to understand the general process.

He grabbed a soda and sat next to his computer in the empty dining room, ready to get this detail taken care of. His grandmother and Margritte had gone to Jackson for the day for doctor's appointments and a shopping excursion, leaving him some peace while he figured the party out. As the days continued to tick by, he felt more and more pressure to hire someone, knowing the reputation of the gala was on the line.

Several of the applications didn't include any pictures of

former events they'd designed, making his life a little easier. He added all those to one folder, cutting it down to fifteen applications. If someone couldn't respond to a direct request on a form, chances were they wouldn't be able to listen to him when he hired them. Birthday parties, baby showers, a wedding reception that was an explosion of flowers. Not all interested him, but he needed someone and fast.

After another perusal of the remaining applications, he was able to cut another four for living more than an hour away. Sure, he was being picky, but he didn't want to pay for someone to live at a hotel while managing all this, and having someone stay in the mansion with them was out of the question. He had to have time to get work done, even if it was in the early morning hours. If the planner stayed at the mansion, he'd never have a moment's peace.

Eleven to go. That was more manageable, and he would be able to get interviews done within a few hours.

Typing out an email to his assistant back in California, he asked that she contact the applicants and set up interviews for the next day. His grandmother had wanted him to work on this, but scheduling the interviews wasn't as important as the actual choosing of the event planner.

What she didn't know right now would be that much easier for him.

* * *

THE NEXT DAY he awoke to more snow. He was just glad he wasn't driving in it on his way up here.

After his run up the hills by the mansion, Dustin was showered and dressed in his suit, ready by nine in the morning for the applicants to arrive for their interviews.

After the first five had come in at their designated times, his hope dipped that he'd ever find someone serious about planning the Christmas Gala. Each of the women had come in more interested in touring the home than actually planning the event.

He'd begun to wonder if his idea to include the tour of the mansion as part of the interview process was a good idea. It allowed the applicants to get an idea for the place so they could give him some ideas for what they would do for the event. Kind of like a pop quiz. Most of them had already forgotten that part and the best description they could give him was "decorate everything in reds and greens, bring in some trees, and hire a caterer."

He was ready to cancel the rest of the interviews and fly someone in from California to plan the party after that last woman. The number of scents coming from her nearly made him gag, and the smells didn't go away for several minutes after she'd left. It would be an extra expense, but he didn't have time to babysit the planner through everything he or she needed to do. And with the Wakefield name on the line, he needed to be sure the planner could deliver.

The doorbell rang again, a few minutes early for the interview. That was the first good sign he'd had all day. When he opened the door, he couldn't help but smile. He hadn't really looked at any of the names on the applications and had only sent out emails to coordinate times for the interview. So seeing the woman from the bank standing on the doorstep made him smile more than he had since he got to Coldwater Creek.

"You," he said.

"Me," she said, giving him a close-lipped smile. She looked as though she'd been expecting to see him, so he must've been right about her discovering who he was. Even though the fire in her eyes blazed, no angry retorts greeted him.

He opened the door and waved her in. "So, you were a teller *and* an event planner?"

She stopped in the small foyer attached to the hallway that led into the main part of the house. He folded his arms and stared at her, watching her squirm a little.

"Not quite yet, but I thought I'd take a leap, you know." Her voice conveyed the defenses rising within her. "If you're going to be like this, though, I've got other things to do." She made a move to reach for the doorknob.

Dustin caught her hand, but a static shock caused him to yank away. He stood back, waving her into the house. "No, you drove up here. I might as well give you a shot, banker girl."

She groaned and shook her head, causing Dustin to smirk. "It's Kassidy, Kassidy McBride. And I don't ever want to be associated with that place again."

Her name clicked as the one the cashier girl had given him at the store on Saturday. "Sounds like there's no love lost there, huh?" Dustin stuck his hands into his suit pants pockets and stared at her, surprised at the light brown of her eyes. For some reason, they reminded him of the root beer barrel candies his grandfather always carried.

They'd stood there for a few seconds when Kassidy said, "Um, did you want to ask me a question?"

She looked more nervous than Dustin had expected from her reaction at the bank, and he wondered if the need to get this job was causing her to tamp down her personality a bit.

"Of course. We'll start with a tour of the house so you'll know what this will entail. You can ask any questions, and then at the end, I'd love to hear what you would do with the place given the opportunity."

Her footfalls were light, making it hard for him to hear her behind him. She followed along as he directed her through the offices, the library, and the giant ballroom on the first floor.

When they rounded back to the dining room where all of his papers and computer sat, he reached his hands out to the side and said, "What do you have for me?"

"Is the second floor not included in the planning of the event?" Kassidy asked, pointing upstairs. Great, she was just like the others. Only here to get a look at the mansion.

"No, we'll be confining it to the first floor." He raised his eyebrows, waiting for her to respond.

She surprised him when she pulled out her phone and started swiping. He was about ready to dismiss her, not willing to put up with being ignored for a phone when he was the one trying to hire someone.

Before he could say anything, she stepped a little closer so he could see the screen.

It was the Clipboard app, and she had several different boards filled with ideas for all holidays and events. As he glanced at the titles of each board, several were already assigned to Christmas themes.

"Here are a few ideas I came up with before seeing the entire floor. But I think going with a classic theme will be the best, to give that feeling of nostalgia. Someone said that last year was all silvers and blues, but that's not Christmas. To me, anyway. Maybe something to do with 'The Twelve Days of Christmas' or *A Christmas Carol*?" She swiped through a few of the images, giving Dustin a sense of what she meant.

"Old school, huh?" he said, trying to gauge her opinion. "You're not all about the modern look?"

She stared into his eyes for several seconds, probably trying to read him.

"I think greens and reds will be just fine for the occasion, and when I'm done, it will wow your guests. We're in a small town in the mountains. Modern doesn't quite fit here."

He smiled, impressed that she didn't try to back down from what she'd planned for this. As the CEO of a major corporation, he'd seen plenty of people backpedal when he questioned what they'd just proposed, even though he agreed with their original proposal. It was the best way to judge their character in business and smaller matters like this.

"Do you have any questions for me?" she asked, tucking her phone back into her jacket.

"How many events have you planned like this?"

Not even flinching, as if she'd prepared herself for this question, she said, "None."

"Why should I pick you to decorate and plan the event?" He tapped his pointer finger over his lips, waiting for her response. The other women he'd interviewed had given him answers he didn't quite believe, like knowledge of the area or an in with a certain company that could provide decorations.

"Mr. Wakefield," Kassidy began.

"Dustin, please."

"I just retired from barrel racing in the last year, and I was fairly successful at it, winning third place at the National Rodeo Finals twice in the last six years. I know what it's like to put in the long hours, to pay attention to the minute changes to make something better. I may not be the most experienced...yet. But I will get there, and with this opportunity, I would put that same dedication into the design process as I would for anything else I do."

Dustin was more than impressed with that answer, but he'd had plenty of years as a boss to know not to let it show just yet. There was still one more question he had for her.

"What happened at the bank, Miss McBride?"

"If I'm calling you Dustin, please call me Kassidy," she said, chuckling a bit. Then her face sobered, and she flicked her eyes away from him for several seconds, as if needing that time to formulate the answer she was going to give him.

"I was passed over for a promotion. And from the information the manager, my former boyfriend, gave me while in his office getting your check signed off, I learned I would probably never be more than a teller while he was in that position." Her eyes bored into him then, holding an intensity he'd rarely seen in people. "I gave him my notice, and I think he'd been preparing for my departure."

"Ex-boyfriend, huh? That would have been interesting to see." He laughed at the glare she gave him.

It said something about her that she hadn't just rolled over and taken it, hoping that sucking up or trying to go above and beyond would change the guy's mind.

"Are you planning to close the factory here in Coldwater Creek?" she asked. From how round her eyes got, it looked like she'd surprised even herself with the question.

He schooled his expression to neutral, just like his grandfather had taught him while growing up. "Where did you hear something like that?"

"It's a small town. Word can get to just about everyone if the right person knows about it." A hint of a smile flickered at the corners of her lips, but her eyes locked onto his, waiting for the answer.

He shrugged and leaned against a wall, trying to ease up some of the tension in the air around them. "You're right about that. And as far as shutting it down, it's not a done deal. It's one of the reasons I came home. I have meetings set up with the managers to talk over problems and figure out what's really going on with the numbers. My grandfather always said you can only know so much from a piece of paper. The rest has to come from seeing things for yourself."

Kassidy's mouth opened slightly, and he could tell she was shocked that he'd even answered her.

"Well, thank you for coming." Dustin stuck his hand out and waited for Kassidy to shake it. A zing of electricity shot between their palms, and Dustin had to work to not jerk his hand back like he'd done earlier when she'd reached for the doorknob. "I'll let you know my decision on the position within the next day."

Kassidy gave him a half-smile. "So if you don't call tomorrow, move on with my life, right?"

Dustin burst out laughing. "Sounds like you've had some experience with that."

"I moved to the city for a while. I had interviews aplenty while I was there. I always appreciated the people who actually sent some kind of message when I didn't get the job. They didn't have to, but it was a courtesy that let me move on to the next thing instead of waiting around forever to hear if the job had been filled or not."

"I will call you either way," Dustin said, leaning against the open door as she walked down the steps to the parking circle. The same forest-green Jeep he'd seen at the bank sat in the driveway.

"Thanks again." Kassidy nodded her head and got in the Jeep, not looking back as she turned around and made her way back down the hill.

She intrigued him more than he wanted to admit. And why was she so angry about the possibility of a factory closure? Had she worked there at some point?

Her directness and preparation were definitely some highlights of the interview. Now he just had another five people to interview. But he had a pretty good idea he had already found the right person for the job.

CHAPTER 7

Kassidy hadn't been this wound up about anything since she'd supposedly tied her rival in a state championship ride at one of the rodeos close to home. Dustin's answers to her questions surprised her, especially the fact that he was so open about the possibility of a closure. But the fact that he would take the time to go to the factory and listen to what was really going on was what struck her the most. It gave him a more personable quality instead of just the stiff CEO she'd taken him for.

Now all she could do was wait for the answer to whether or not she got the job.

"What are you cleaning now?" her mother asked, walking into the upstairs bathroom.

Kassidy raised an old toothbrush from where she'd been scrubbing around the base of the toilet. "Your sons are disgusting, by the way," she said, raising a lip in disgust.

"You don't have to tell me that. I've been cleaning around toilets since I potty-trained Easton all those years ago. You'd think they would know by now to clean it up themselves."

She stepped into the bathroom and sat on the edge of the tub. "Still haven't heard back yet, huh?"

Kassidy did everything she could to keep from glancing at her phone again in the hopes that maybe she'd missed the call or something. If Dustin Wakefield kept his word and even bothered to call her. But then again, the way he'd said it made her think he would keep his word.

The last twenty-four hours had been near torturous. The waiting was killing her because if by some chance she did get the job, she'd have to cram three months' worth of planning into three weeks.

She'd run down the battery on her phone from just turning the screen on and off all day, but she'd never wanted something more than this chance at a new career, one she could create on her own and not from following Walker's footsteps and joining the rodeo.

"Nothing yet. I just figured I'd stay busy."

"You've more than done that if you're on the floor in the bathroom. What if we head into town? I need to get some things for the youth activity I'm in charge of tomorrow, and it might be good for you to see outside the four walls of our house."

Kassidy tossed the toothbrush down and grinned. "Yes! Please, let's go do something."

Her mom chuckled, and Kassidy headed into her room to grab the plaid jacket she'd bought last year. It was one of the warmest things she owned, and she loved the print.

"Ready," she said, heading down the stairs a couple at a time.

"You're not going to change out of your old jeans?" her mom asked, pointing to the paint-splattered pair Kassidy had donned.

Kassidy shrugged. "I don't think we'll see anyone anyway. I'll be fine."

Famous last words.

Twenty minutes later, they walked into the small drugstore, veering to the small section of craft supplies. They'd tried the town's slightly larger craft store first, only to find a note that the owner was at her son's wrestling match at the high school and had closed the shop early. One of the downsides to living in a town so small.

"Is that all you need?" Kassidy asked, her arms full of glue and pipe cleaners.

"I think so. Ooo, there's some of those mints you like. Let's get some." Her mother grabbed the package of small chocolate mints Kassidy bought when she needed a little pick-me-up.

"You don't think I got the job, do you?" Kassidy said, a slight whine in her voice. Her mother was the fount of all positivity. If she didn't believe Kassidy would get the job, then Kassidy's hopes would be dashed even before she heard the final decision from Wakefield Mansion.

"I just think we shouldn't give up yet. There are still a few hours left in the day. Maybe he got busy and hasn't made a decision yet."

Kassidy dropped the items onto the counter next to the register and covered her face with her hands. "I don't know why I even thought I had a chance."

Her mother tugged at Kassidy's wrists, pulling her hands away. "Because you are an amazing event planner, and I can only imagine how that interview went. If anything, he doesn't hire you because you were too persuasive."

"That makes me feel so much better, Mom," Kassidy said, rolling her eyes.

Her mother laughed, and they both turned to the cashier who was giving them an odd smile.

Once the order was rung up and paid for, Kassidy and her mom trudged out of the store. Kassidy glanced up at the parking lot, her eyes locking on a familiar car pulling into a parking space. Two spots over from her mom's SUV.

"Umm...did you forget anything?" Kassidy asked, grabbing her mom's wrist and trying to turn her back inside the store. But as usual for Tonya McBride, she put up a fight, twisting her arm enough that Kassidy let go.

"What is wrong with you?" her mom asked through gritted teeth.

Kassidy turned her back to the parking lot and leaned closer. "Mr. Wakefield just pulled into the parking lot."

She'd just run into him at the grocery store on Saturday, when he'd rammed his cart into her leg. And now he was coming to the drugstore? If only she could find a way to not see him, because she knew this hope she'd had of working at the mansion would be killed just by seeing pity on Dustin's perfect face.

A light breeze brushed against her cheek, and she turned to find her mother walking in the direction of the car. "Come on, Kassidy. Now's your chance."

Kassidy turned around and started after her mother, when Dustin made an appearance, walking in their direction. His usually crisp attire looked a little worse for wear, with his tie loosened around his neck and his dress shirt wrinkled in front. Despite the cold weather, he hadn't buttoned up his coat.

He smiled when he saw her, and Kassidy paused, feeling like her legs might give out from under her. And there she stood in her painted jeans and her hair in a messy bun. At least she'd looked more professional yesterday for the interview.

"Chance for what?" he asked, pausing next to the car where her mother had popped the trunk.

"Um, well, a chance to beat her to the car." The excuse sounded lame to her own ears.

"Hi, I'm Tonya McBride," Kassidy's mom said, reaching out her hand.

Dustin took it and shook, staring at her mother's face with a slight smile.

"I was good friends with your father back in the day. I'm so sorry for your loss."

The smile left his face, and his Adam's apple bobbed a few times. "Thank you. It's been a long time, but there are still moments when it's painful."

The vulnerability in his expression caused Kassidy to study his features too closely. His jawline was strong, and the color of his eyes seemed to be a bit more green at the moment than the turquoise she'd noticed yesterday and at the bank.

"Kassidy tells me you're in charge of the Wakefield Christmas Gala this year. I'm sure the town will be so excited for whatever you come up with."

Dustin nodded, avoiding Kassidy's gaze for several seconds before glancing over at her. "I was going to call earlier, but I've had a massive headache and thought I'd venture down for some ibuprofen and cold medicine before it gets worse."

Kassidy barely breathed, some strange part of her subconscious telling her that if she did anything to distract him, she wouldn't get the job.

"There were a few applicants with better qualifications," he said.

Hope withered in her chest. Of course. Why had she even thought this was possible?

"But I wanted to extend you the offer of getting the mansion ready for the holidays. There will be a lot of celebrities and other people coming, so just keep that in mind." He glanced around the dim parking lot, the last rays of the sun shining over the mountains to the west. "Sorry, I'm usually more formal when extending a job offer, but all the finer details will have to wait until morning. If you accept, that is."

Kassidy was stunned, not sure what to think of actually landing her dream job.

Her mother nudged her, motioning to Dustin with her head to get Kassidy to talk.

"Oh, um, of course. Thank you so much." Kassidy's voice sounded robotic as she tried to comprehend the excitement and the enormity of the task ahead. "When would you like me to start?"

"How about you drop by the house tomorrow morning. I have a conference call starting at ten, but sometime before that would be good. We can get all the papers signed and go over the contract. Will that work?"

Words had never had a problem coming to her before, but at the moment, Kassidy was speechless. She nodded, forcing a smile through the disbelief that she'd gotten the offer.

"Perfect. I'll see you then." He nodded to Kassidy and turned to her mother. "It was a pleasure meeting you. Have a good night." He waved to the two of them and strolled into the drug store.

Was that really the guy who'd interviewed her yesterday? There was something very different about him, but then again, a crushing headache could do that to a person.

Kassidy turned to her mother, the shock finally wearing off, and leaned in for a giant hug. "Thank you for nudging me, like always."

"What are mothers for?" her mom said with a grin. "I'm so proud of you and excited for this chance. If you need any help, you know I'll be here."

"Thanks, Mom. I'm sure I'll be taking you up on that at some point."

They got into the SUV, and her mom shifted the car into

reverse. "So where will you start? Do you have an idea of what you'll do?"

"I'll need to do some measurements and figure out a flow for the party, but I can do that in the morning. Right now, I'll just have to start clipping things to my boards so I have a better idea when I get there tomorrow." She paused a moment. "I can't believe he picked me over the others who had more experience."

Heat rushed up her cheeks as she thought about what she'd said to him when she arrived the day before. She'd let her hot-headed temper through, and she wondered if it had helped her get the job or if maybe her ideas for what to do for the party had been the right answer.

At least she got it. She breathed out a sigh of relief and sank back against the passenger seat. She'd be able to pay the bills for the next few months.

"You might want to get a website up and going tonight. Maybe find a logo you like for your company," her mom said, glancing over with a wide smile.

"Company? This is my second job, ever. First one that pays, though."

"Kass, there will be celebrities there. When you pull this off with a bang, which you will, you'll have clients flooding in to book your services. Why not set things up from the beginning?"

"I know nothing about websites, Mom."

"No, but Lauren was saying the gal taking over for them at the lodge while she and Walker are on vacation is some big-time blogger. Ashley something. Maybe give her a call and see if she has any insight."

Kassidy frowned. "You want me to call up some girl I don't even know and say, 'Hey, will you design my website?' That's not going to work."

Her mother leaned over and patted her leg. "Oh, Kass, I

wasn't saying to just dump it into her lap. Maybe we could swing by and check on things at the lodge for a few minutes. You could ask who she recommends for building websites."

Tonya McBride wasn't going to let her get off easy, so Kassidy said, "I did tell Lauren we'd grab that one broken frame so Colter can fix it. May as well stop on the way home." She tried to play off the fact that she cared about the idea of creating a business, but this was the most excited she'd been about anything since she'd decided to head to California at the beginning of the year.

So much had happened with just a few words from Dustin, telling her she'd gotten the job. Now she just needed to follow through and make it the most memorable gala ever.

CHAPTER 8

Dustin chuckled as he replayed the expression on Kassidy's face after he told her she had the job. The last few interviews had been interesting, and he hadn't lied when he said there were a couple of planners with more experience, but neither had come with ideas already planned out for him. Kassidy had already done some of the legwork for the job, and from the passion she'd shown him, he knew she'd deliver.

"That will be fifteen sixty-seven."

Dustin handed the cashier a twenty-dollar bill and thanked him, refusing the change. He wasn't even out the door before he'd popped open the bottle of ibuprofen and swallowed a couple of them with a long gulp of cola. The height of the pain was still growing, but he hoped the medicine would curb the length of it somewhat.

Getting back to the mansion, he was grateful his grandma had already gone to bed. The intensity of the pain behind his eyes made it hard to function, the spots at the periphery of his vision signaling that he wasn't past the migraine. He fell into bed, ready to sleep it off in the pitch-black room.

When he finally woke up, the pain had receded some, but there was still a halo around his vision. Checking his phone, he did a double-take, seeing it was nearly nine the next morning.

He was supposed to be on with headquarters back in California in an hour, and he still had a couple more reports to go through. The main topic for the meeting was to talk about the details and fate of the factory here in Coldwater Creek. He'd come back to Coldwater Creek determined to shut it down because of the lower production numbers, but after going over the reports, he needed to see the factory itself, to talk to the people and get their explanations for how things were.

It was something his grandfather had always prided himself on doing, visiting the factories from time to time to get a better in-depth take on how the factories and the employees were actually running. It was something he needed to get back to doing.

The doorbell rang, and he took a quick look in the mirror. The rumpled suit pants he'd forgotten to change out of as the fury of the migraine took over last night and his hair sticking up on one side caused him to groan. He usually didn't sleep this long even with a headache coming on.

Running a comb through his hair, he assumed Margritte would get the door. But when the bell rang again, he knew he'd have to be okay with the disheveled look for a few minutes. He hurried downstairs, buttoning his shirt along the way.

With a quick twist of the knob, he opened the door, surprised to see Kassidy on the front step. Their conversation floated back to his mind from the night before. He'd told her to come over in the morning, and now he was flustered. He'd always taken such care to keep everything in his life buttoned up.

Memories of opening up to Lila washed over him. He thought he loved her, had even bought a ring for her, until she saw he wasn't completely perfect and hated going to all the major functions she did—and redirected her interest to his best friend.

Using his fingers to comb through his hair, he waved Kassidy in. "Go ahead and have a seat at the table. I need to change, and I'll be right back."

"Are you okay?" Kassidy asked, concern pulling her eyebrows together.

He waved her away, already a few steps up the stairs. "Yeah, just had to sleep off the headache last night. I'll go change, and we'll get things all filled out."

After a two-minute shower, he realized he'd forgotten to take his suits to the cleaners. Not that he'd absolutely need them to interview people over the computer, but it had become some kind of security blanket. After donning a polo and some slacks, he came down the stairs and was surprised by the amount of stuff she'd brought with her.

"Did you just haul that in from your Jeep? Where did you find all this stuff?" Dustin asked her, pointing to a book of fabric and then a ring of paint swatches.

"Yes. I borrowed the paint book from the hardware store, and the fabric is from Lottie's fabric store. My mom has wooed many a person in this town with her apple pie. I may have benefitted from a recent manic baking episode."

Dustin chuckled and took a seat catty-corner from Kassidy. He pushed over a packet of paper toward her, followed by a pen. "Okay, here is the contract between Wakefield Family Trust and yourself. Or your company if you have one."

She reached over, her fingers wrapping around the top of the pen. Her pinky skimmed his knuckle, sending a tingle along his skin toward the back of his hand. He glanced up, studying her face. Had she felt it too?

A broad smile appeared along with a twinkle in her eye. "I actually do. Rustic Event Planning. A friend helped me come up with it last night."

When she smiled like that, Dustin wondered why he'd sworn off women.

"Perfect. Okay, here are the terms. Your employment for the Wakefield Family begins once you sign those papers and will end when the gala is over, or whenever the Wakefield family no longer needs your services."

A shadow crossed her expression, but it was gone before he could say anything, making him wonder if he'd just made it up in the first place. This was business, something his grandmother should have been here to handle. He couldn't worry about her emotions, even though he wanted to.

He forged on, trying to regain his usual CEO composure as he spoke to her. "We will give you a notice if anything isn't up to what we usually prefer standard-wise, but I wouldn't have hired you for this if I didn't think you could follow through and succeed."

"No pressure, right?" Kassidy said, appearing more over-whelmed than she had before.

She flipped through the pages, scanning several sections before signing on the three pages near the end. Dustin tried not to smile as he saw the hearts drawn above the i's in her name.

"I'll scan it and email you a copy for your records." He looked down at the list of things he'd wanted to talk to her about, but as he stared at the words written, he realized that would be micromanaging a little more than he wanted to be.

He set the paper on the other side of his laptop and glanced back at her, staring into the milk-chocolate eyes that were pulling him in, threatening to unsettle the wall he'd built around his heart. "Any questions from you?"

"What is the budget for the project? It looks like some things need freshened up, and if I need to work with any contractors to fix anything, will I need to work that into the budget? Or will you take that from a different account?"

"Good question," he said, wagging his pointer finger in her direction. "Let's just make the budget you're working with for decorations, food, and entertainment. If you find things that need to be fixed throughout the house, let me know and we'll find someone to take care of it."

Kassidy nodded, checking off a few things in the notebook she was holding. "Okay, is there anything that should not be in the final display? Anything you and your grandmother don't like?"

"We're pretty flexible when it comes to celebrations, but I'll think about that and get back to you with anything I come up with. My grandmother will have a list of the attendees, usually people we work with or have contracts with, so if you need to nail down numbers, you'll have to ask her." He tapped his pointer finger against his lips, trying to remember anything he'd missed. "Oh, and just make sure to get a half-gallon of the whole chocolate milk for Santa to drink."

He winked at her, and she frowned.

"Sorry, I should have known you haven't…" He trailed off, feeling the awkwardness of the situation. Only a few of the families from the valley had ever come to the gala, usually the ones related to the high-up managers. "Well, it's kind of a tradition that the Santa Claus who comes to visit at the Wakefield Gala gets whole chocolate milk because of the number of dairy farms in the valley." He tried to read her expression.

"I'd never heard that before," she said, leaning over to write milk in her notebook. The swoop of her hand as she made the letters and the neatness of them caused Dustin to smile. He'd always had the worst handwriting, probably because he was in a hurry to get it all written down before he forgot.

She glanced back up at him. "Okay, I'll ask you if I have any other questions."

Dustin nodded, staring longer than he should have. His gaze flicked between her eyes and lips. The moment his mind started to wonder what kissing her would be like, he broke his gaze away and stood, needing to busy himself with anything at the moment—anything but the girl who was slowly breaking down the walls he'd erected for himself.

"Don't you have a conference call right now?" she asked, pointing to the computer in front of him.

He startled out of his trance and looked at the grandfather clock he'd wound up a few days ago. Two minutes until he was supposed to be set up.

"Uh, yeah. Thanks for the reminder." He stepped over to the seat in front of the computer and powered it on, watching as Kassidy pulled out a measuring tape and started taking measurements of the room.

There was one thing he liked, and that was someone who was thorough. She might not have had a ton of experience, but something about her told him she would get the job done.

Something had changed between them. He just hoped it wasn't because she felt she needed to get on his good side since he'd given her the job.

CHAPTER 9

Kassidy spent more than two hours taking measurements of the rooms just on the first floor. Her notebook filled up quickly with general notes of how she wanted to decorate each room, and the number of new pictures on her camera roll reached over two hundred. She hoped her old computer had enough space to upload them.

Sure, it took a lot of time to get the boards on her Clipboard app all set up with the pictures and information on the room, but she hoped it would help her keep things organized and know exactly how much of each material she needed to buy. Three weeks wasn't much when it came to planning an event like this, but she couldn't start doubting now.

She ran her finger across an end table near the entry of one of the rooms, the shine not quite to the level she wanted. Adding polish to her list, she started measuring the room next to the dining room, where every cell in her body was fully aware that Dustin was on the other side of the wall. She couldn't like him, couldn't even begin to understand what his life was like: losing his parents so young, being raised by his grandparents, and now taking over a very lucrative business. And yet, when she'd brushed his finger and he'd locked eyes with her, she'd had to hold back a shiver.

The man was attractive, dreamily so. But he was just a guy passing through, not set to stay in this small town for longer than the holiday.

It made her simple life here in Coldwater Creek seem small.

"I don't want to go that route, Jeff, if we don't have to. Show me the spreadsheet with all those numbers again." Dustin's voice betrayed irritation, and Kassidy could relate. If she had to deal with too many people too often, things wouldn't go well for her or a business.

As she started thinking about the schedule she'd need to have for this project, she also needed to think of a few people she could call on for help, especially with the decorating part of it. It wouldn't be easy to hang the heavy garlands all by herself once the time came.

Again, Dustin's voice interrupted her mental schedule.

"Okay, those numbers aren't awful, but they aren't good either," he said, a bit louder this time. "Yeah, I know it would be easier just to close it up, but I need hard, factual evidence before we make any definitive decision."

Was he talking about closing the plant? Her stomach turned and she hoped he was talking about something completely different. She poked her head around the corner, studying him for a moment as he stared at the screen of the computer.

His light brown hair wasn't perfectly in place like it had been every other time she'd seen him. And those crazy blueish-greenish eyes seemed to change with what he wore. When he smiled, which was rare, it lit up his whole face, making him look ten times more attractive than when he was studying something.

She ducked behind the wall again when he glanced her way, embarrassed that she'd been caught checking him out.

What was her problem? She'd been one of the toughest competitors at the rodeo just a year ago, and now she was turning into a puddle over a guy who probably looked at her as though she'd just come out of the horse stall with manure on her boots.

Sure, he'd been polite, but there was a formality that blocked him off from her. And rightly so. He was her boss now, for the next couple of months at least. And how could she forget how her last relationship with her boss had gone?

Focus on the work.

By the time she'd finished getting all the pictures and measurements, she ducked out of the house, not wanting to disturb him as his voice rose in a heated discussion about the number of employees at the plant. Her insides twisted as she thought of how real getting closed down could be. One factory closed would send ripple effects for years to come.

It would be hard to run a company as big as Wakefield Fabrication, and Kassidy was glad all she had to do was the more glamorous part of putting on a party.

From what she'd learned about Dustin Wakefield so far, he definitely didn't fit the complete version of a recluse, just a work-driven man who probably didn't get out much because of his job.

There were some things the gossipers tended to get right, but when it came to the guy who hadn't lived here in over a decade, she'd just have to wait and see.

By the time he got off the call, Dustin was wound up and ready for a fight. There were so many moving parts to the fabrication business, and he needed all of them moving in sync to make an impact on the bottom line of the company.

One of the locations in Utah had run out of materials because their supplies director had left to have a baby the month before and the head manager hadn't replaced her since then. Poor management affected more than just that one area, and with all the time off the company allowed for the holiday toward the end of December, Dustin didn't need employees standing around bored because they didn't have the materials to create the products they were assigned.

He stood and stretched, walking around to see if Kassidy was still there. He'd wanted to talk to her more, to make up something to talk to her about, but the call had gone much longer than he'd planned.

As he rounded a corner, he caught a light whiff of her perfume, a floral scent he couldn't place. To be honest, he hadn't been around a woman younger than his grandmother in a handful of years, and this wasn't a heavy scent.

What was it about this woman that felt like it exposed his reclusiveness? There were women who worked at the offices in California, but they reminded him of bunnies, stating the things that needed to be said and hopping away quickly as if he were some kind of wolf.

He spotted a paper on the ground and walked over to pick it up. It looked like the measurements she'd taken for several of the rooms. She'd probably be needing it if she were to begin ordering decorations. He could keep it for the next time she came by, but then again, he wasn't sure when that would be.

The clock chimed one in the afternoon. He could use a distraction before the managers of the Coldwater Creek plant got back to him. It would've been easier to drive the twenty minutes to the plant to demand the paperwork, but he would be there in a few days anyway, and he hoped to keep out of the spotlight until a final decision had been made.

Dustin headed upstairs to grab the pile of dirty suits and then back down to jump in the Maserati. Getting them to the dry cleaner was a must, and then he could go for a burger down at the diner.

As he shifted the car into reverse, he glanced over at the slightly crumpled paper with Kassidy's neat penmanship on the passenger seat. On his way home, if he could think of a good reason as to why he didn't leave it at the house, he'd drop by Kassidy's house with the paper.

He'd just need to think that one through while he filled his stomach.

* * *

DUSTIN SPENT lunch trying to focus on the hamburger he hadn't tasted in years. The small drive-in diner had burgers that beat all the ones he'd ever tried in California.

Several people turned in his direction as he focused on dunking the fries into the fry sauce the people of this town made in buckets. He could hear them whispering, "Isn't that the Wakefield boy?" and, "The Wakefield grandson." A few minutes ticked by, and he'd just finished the dregs of his strawberry shake when someone whispered, "Is he here to close the plant?"

Scrunching the napkin in his hand, he stood, dropping his garbage into the designated bins and walking out the door.

He wished he was used to this, that being the head of a major corporation for four years had given him thicker skin to insulate from what people were saying about him. Instead, the self-doubt came rushing in.

He'd worked for years to overcome those lingering thoughts of inadequacy brought on by the expectations of so many people in this valley, and by his grandfather's expectations until he'd passed on. And again as his limited experience was questioned over and over by the employees underneath him.

Winding the car around some of the curves, he tried to think through the problems at the local plant. He'd only closed one other plant since he'd taken over, and that he hadn't taken lightly. People and their families were always affected by those kinds of big decisions, and that kind of news this close to Christmas would be devastating on the valley.

It took nearly a minute to figure out where he'd driven while focused on work, the surroundings throwing him a bit. He had a sense of déjà vu, but searching his memories, he couldn't remember driving in this area. The sky grew dark, the white clouds from earlier now a dark gray.

That's just what he didn't need, a snowstorm to hit the valley. He'd all but forgotten how to drive in the snow.

A wooden arch rose up, and he read the sign on top: *McBride Ranch.*

He stared down the long stretch of road lined with a few pine trees. Once those ended, a large cabin came into view, accented by the mountains as a backdrop. It wasn't as big as some of the places he'd stayed, but it was well-kept and everything looked taken care of.

He stared at the lights through the windows as he pulled up to the house, wondering for a moment which room was Kassidy's. Throwing the car into park, he paused. What was he doing? He wasn't some high school kid who could just go up to the door and say, "Hey, is Kassidy home?"

He was her boss. And he didn't date his employees. Not after the second-biggest betrayal of his life when he'd been with Cynthia Carlisle. She'd been one of the VPs in his company, and they'd gone out together whenever he was in Colorado. Until he found out she was actually engaged to some guy from her hometown. Why didn't people just tell the truth up front?

And then Lila. Yeah, he wasn't going there.

Putting the car into reverse, he was about to back down the driveway when the front door opened and Kassidy stepped out, looking both concerned and nervous.

He stopped the car. He couldn't just drive away now. He'd been spotted, and from the look on her face, he wanted to make sure she was okay.

He pulled forward, putting the car into park and opening his door.

Kassidy came down the steps, the frown line in her forehead scaring him just a bit. "What are you doing here?" she asked, cocking her head to the side and giving him a forced smile.

"You forgot this paper, and I, uh, I just wanted to make sure you got it."

She stepped forward and took the paper from his hand, their fingers brushing as she did so. Dustin felt that zip of electricity crackle between them before she broke her gaze away from him and looked down at the paper.

"Oh, thank you. You didn't have to bring it all the way here, though. I could've picked it up the next time I was at your house."

And that's why he shouldn't have come. Maybe he was feeling something she wasn't. That sounded just like him.

He shrugged, trying to look unaffected. "I was in town to get some dinner and figured I'd bring it by."

Her chuckle was nervous, and she said, "I thought you'd come to fire me already."

Dustin relaxed somewhat. "Oh, uh, yeah. I mean, no. You haven't done enough to know if I should fire you or not." He winced, wishing he could have made it sound more like a joke than a threat.

A crack of thunder sounded overhead, and he jumped, not expecting it.

"Are you scared of thunder?" she asked, her smile returning.

"No." He chuckled, wishing he'd just gone straight home. This was nearly unbearable. "Well, I better get back before the storm hits. I'll, uh, see you soon, I guess."

"Drive safe," she said, her voice a little more tender compared to the other things they'd talked about in the last two minutes. She stood there and watched him back out, waving once he got to the end of the drive.

Why did his feelings have to surface now? And what was he going to do about his rule to never date an employee? Or date any woman, period?

CHAPTER 11

"Who was that outside, Kass?" her father asked as she walked back in, paper in hand.

"Dustin Wakefield. He brought me the paper of the measurements I'd taken of the rooms today."

Kassidy stepped into the kitchen and slipped the paper into the notebook she'd been working on for the last few hours, since she'd returned from the Wakefield estate. There were so many things to cover and get ordered that she figured she'd better start now.

"Well, that was nice of him, don't you think?" her mother said with a wink. She was stirring something in one of the large pots, and it already smelled delicious. Something with garlic and onions.

"Sure, it was nice," Kassidy said out loud.

She wasn't sure what to make of the gesture. Dustin seemed so abrupt, and sometimes cold, about everything. But then he took time out of his afternoon and drove to her house, in the opposite direction from his own, to drop off a piece of paper.

The romantic part of her wanted to run wild, swooning

that he'd just wanted to see her again. But reality swept in, telling her that he'd left too hastily to even make it worth anything. Maybe he was just an analytical guy who was worried about the gala going off without a hitch for his grandmother's sake and thought she'd need to get going on the preparations. He seemed every bit the workaholic she's already suspected. She just hoped he wouldn't expect her to be one as well.

Anytime she hoped things could be possible in the future, she remembered that he was debating the closure of the plant. Sure, he might take bald facts into consideration by meeting there at the plant, but Wakefield Fabrication hadn't gotten to where it was without keeping decisions all about business.

It was just hard to think that hundreds, if not thousands, of lives would be affected by his final decision. The factory was more than a collection of facts. It would be easier to keep her heart wrapped up than to have it broken when the decision was final and he left town.

"How do you like working for him, Kass?" her father asked over the top of his newspaper. It was later than his usual time to read through everything the local town had going on, but he'd been up early helping Easton with some cattle that got stuck on another piece of property across the creek.

"Well, it hasn't been bad over the past two days. He's very…efficient when he talks to me. I used to think there was no way someone could be tired from working behind a computer. But I think he's mentioned at least three conference calls he's had to make just in the time I was there." Kassidy took a sip of water from the cup she'd filled at lunch, allowing her to ponder her father's question a little more. "I'm just glad it's not me."

"Busy man. But I bet you'll be good for him, to loosen him up."

Kassidy's mouth dropped open. "What's that supposed to mean?"

Her father looked like he was trying to keep from smiling or laughing by opening his mouth wide, stuttering out a defense. "I'm just saying that you're usually one to find the fun. Maybe he could use a little help with that as well."

Kassidy shook her head. "He's my boss, Dad. We all remember how things turned out with Trace." She paused, tilting her head a bit to make sure he knew she was serious. "And I'm not sure I want to get involved in a friendship if he's going to just move back to LA after the holidays, which it sounds like that's his plan."

"There are ways of making him stick around," her dad purred.

"David!" Kassidy's mom said in shock. "She's trying to establish a career, not woo the man."

"Thank you, Mom," Kassidy said, feeling grateful she had at least one parent on her side. She couldn't help but add, "Although, we're not in a Jane Austen novel."

Her mother tossed a wadded-up label at her. "Well, he is attractive. Maybe a little distraction would help him see how important this valley is. Keep him around a while."

There went all the sympathy.

Kassidy picked up her notebook and computer, tucking them under her arm. She schooled her face to keep the leap of excitement at their words from showing on her face. She had to be crazy to even think there could ever be a possibility of something between her and Dustin.

"I'm not dating him or anyone, all right? I've got to get working on this, so I'll see you later." She turned and ran up the stairs to the loft, hoping her parents wouldn't notice just how red her cheeks were.

"Dinner will be ready in thirty," her mother reminded her as she hit the top stair.

Kassidy flopped down on her bed and opened up the ClipBoard app. Hopefully, working on the gala would be enough to get stray thoughts of kissing Dustin Wakefield out of her mind.

CHAPTER 12

It felt like forever since Kassidy had been tubing down the slopes with her family. They'd missed a few years because of the NFR and the craziness of the holiday season, but with the new snowfall lasting Thursday night into all day Friday, there wasn't a better opportunity than that Saturday.

Guilt welled up as she thought of all she still needed to do to organize for the gala, but she wanted—no, needed—to do something physical to keep from going crazy trying to keep track of everything she'd decided on and the things she still needed to do for the gala.

She glanced out at the countryside as she sat in the back of the truck on the trip up the hill. One of the homeowners who lived up the old country road would pack the snow down after a storm, allowing the people from around town to enjoy the perfectly straight road with plenty of incline.

Pulling the sleds out of the back of the truck, she made sure everyone had what they needed.

"Just get on your sled, Mother Hen," Hunter said, laughing at her. It was just her brothers, younger sister, and

Lauren who'd made the trek up the mountain that early morning. Their dad was in charge of the drop-off truck that was heading down the snow-packed road at the moment.

She scrunched her nose and rolled her eyes at him. The twins got away with murder when their mom was around, but Kassidy called them out on their shenanigans enough that they were always giving her a hard time.

Glancing down at the sled she was left with, she realized a large crack ran along the side and down the middle of the sled from the previous run.

"Okay, who broke the sled?" she demanded. No one met her eyes until she turned toward the other twin, Colter. "You had it last time. I get that one."

"Um, no," he said, pushing off and heading down the hill.

"Get in, Kass," Easton said, scooting to the back of his sled. Luckily, it was a double-rider, but there was very little room up front for her in addition to his bulky frame.

"Go!" Walker called out, racing next to his wife down the hill.

Easton and Kassidy pushed off, the weight of both of them causing it to speed along the snow, closing the distance from the other sleds.

They picked up even more speed right as they were supposed to stop at the bottom of the hill where their father had parked the truck.

"Looks like we're going through," Easton yelled.

Kassidy looked both ways, grateful that the road wasn't busy or they'd crash.

They flew through and caught some air in the process, heading down the next hill, the momentum carrying them up to the crest of the next one with ease. It was shorter than the initial hill they'd come down, but Kassidy had never made it this far in one run. The sled still had plenty of speed when she turned and saw a dark car coming in their direction.

"Is he going to stop?" Kassidy yelled, hoping it would somehow alert the driver to them.

A few feet before the intersection, she felt the sled tilt to the side, sliding them off into the ditch instead of continuing on their path forward into the intersecting road.

A screech of tires sounded, and Kassidy knew it would've been too late if her brother hadn't veered them off course.

A car door opened and shut as Kassidy worked to step through the hip-high snow, trying to get back to the road.

"Are you all right?" a familiar voice called down.

She didn't have to look up to know it was Dustin Wakefield. Why did he keep showing up everywhere she was?

"We're fine. Just went a little farther than we thought." Easton had already managed to get back to the snow-packed road, the long sled under his arm.

Kassidy made it almost to the edge and then tripped, falling face-first into the powder. The cold of it took her breath away, and when she resurfaced, she took large gulps, swiping at the snow on her face with her already covered gloves, making it even worse.

By the time she could see, a hand was reaching out to her.

She glanced up to see Dustin squatted down in a nice peacoat and expensive shoes. She stared at his hand for several seconds before taking it. He was going to get wet and snowed on, but at this point, she just wanted out of the ditch.

"Thank you," she said, brushing off the rest of the snow so she didn't have to make eye contact.

"You're welcome." He smiled, looking between her and Easton. "What are you up to?"

"We're just sledding." She hoped her quick answer would give him the hint to get back into his car and move on. Her twin brothers hadn't stopped giving her a hard time about working for her former crush, and she didn't need them to see him rescuing her now.

"That hill over there is where we start. One of us drives the rest to the top and then we slide down," Easton said.

Dustin turned in the direction Easton pointed, where their family stood waiting by the truck. His surprise was only slight, but it was there all the same. "Looks like you went a distance farther than normal, huh?"

Easton chuckled, and Kassidy forced a smile. She had hoped to have at least one day free of this guy, or of the thought of this guy and the job she was supposed to perform for him.

"You should join us," Easton said, ever the party crasher. "We've got a few extra snow clothes up there if you want to try it out. You're Dustin Wakefield, Kassidy's boss, right? I'm Easton, Kassidy's oldest brother." He reached out his hand. "I think you were a couple years younger in school. You probably know Walker, our brother."

At the mention of his boss title, Kassidy could feel her already bright pink cheeks heat up, probably more of a bright red at this point.

"Nice to meet you, but I should probably be going," he said, locking eyes with Kassidy.

"Oh, yeah. You're always working. I'm sure you've got another conference call or something coming up." She bit the end of her tongue, feeling guilty that she'd been sharp to her boss. But then again, that was kind of how they'd met for this whole adventure, with her telling him off.

He glanced in the direction of the hill again and then at her, his smile widening as he stared at her. "Looks like fun. If you've got some extra clothes, I'll give it a try." A challenge in his eyes caused a strange twist in her stomach.

"Sweet! Just meet us on the next road. You can park down

at the bottom where our truck is sitting right now." Easton waved and started trekking back up the hill.

Kassidy did what she could to catch up to him, her snow boots heavy and slipping on the snowy road. "We already don't have enough sleds, and you invite him?" Why couldn't he have just let him move on?

"Why not? Like you said, he works a lot. Sometimes a break can help people chill out." Easton flashed her a smile. "I did it to help you, sis."

Kassidy punched him in the shoulder with all the strength she had. "Yeah, right. You just like to see me squirm."

She was breathing heavily once they made it back to the truck. Everyone else had loaded their sleds and were waiting for them to come.

"We need some of the extra gear. We've got a new addition to the fun," Easton said, laughing when Kassidy shot him a look of disgust again.

"Who?" Hunter and Colter asked at the same time.

"Looks like Kassidy's boss," Walker said, wrapping his arms around Lauren. A stab of envy shot through Kassidy at the sight of the two of them all cozy together.

She turned around to find Dustin doing his best to move up the hill, slipping the whole way in his leather shoes.

"Now would be the time to help out," Easton said, whispering in her ear. Was he crazy? Had he hit his head on the way down that last run? The twins would have a field day with her helping Dustin on the hill, and she was doing her best to avoid him for several reasons.

Letting out an internal sigh, she stepped down the hill about fifty feet and reached out her hand to Dustin, who grabbed it and took small steps as she pulled him up the short distance to the truck.

Once they arrived, the truck pulled away, leaving a small pile of snow clothes and gear.

"Really, guys?" she said, her hands outstretched. If this was some kind of sabotage or intervention to get her to interact more with the billionaire, she wasn't amused.

"Looks like they were excited to go down again, huh?" Dustin asked, blowing into his hands. They were already pink from the cold.

Kassidy didn't answer that, only stepped toward the mound and pulled out a pair of snow pants. She pulled up the tag and said, "Will a medium work?" She glanced over his body as he removed his coat. He wore khaki pants and a button-up shirt with a tie that all seemed to fit just perfectly, showing off the trim figure.

Breaking her gaze away, she bent down and searched for another pair. "Here's a large. I think that's the best we've got for these."

"That might work. We'll see." He stepped into them with each leg before pulling up the suspenders. He had to tug a few times to get the pieces to latch over his shoulder, but at least he was covered.

"Do you come here often?" he asked, tugging on the second strap.

"Look who's chatty now," Kassidy said, teasing. She nodded. "Whenever we get enough snow that the road is packed down. Last year we had a ton of snow but it didn't stick to the road very well. And my siblings were all busy with their own lives and relationships that we just didn't make it over."

"These are all your siblings?" he asked, glancing up the road. The truck was just inching its way back down, and the sleds would be following soon.

"Yeah, and one sister-in-law. My oldest two brothers just got married this year."

Dustin sifted through a few more items and pulled out a coat. "I probably shouldn't ask, but why do you have this many extra pieces of snow gear when you're all dressed?" He waved up and down his body as he put on the hoodie and grabbed a beanie and a pair of gloves. A pair of old snow boots actually slid on without any extra tugging and pulling. The colors were all over the place, and she was surprised that a guy who took great pride in his everyday appearance would be okay with the mismatched look.

"Sometimes it's cold; sometimes we lose things or they tear. And to be honest, I think my dad just forgets to take things out of his truck. Once it's in there, it stays until my mom makes him clean it out."

As they turned and watched the sledders coming down the hill, Kassidy studied him in her periphery. She didn't need to take extra notice of him, knowing a good part of her future depended on whether or not he was closing the factory. But she liked the fact that he was more relaxed than when she'd met him at the bank that first day.

Once Kassidy's siblings made it down to the bottom, they loaded back up, joking about Colter sliding right into one of the snowbanks. Sleds were placed in the truck bed, with some of the sledders hanging off the tailgate of the truck.

Somehow Dustin and Kassidy were sitting together, and she felt an odd sort of zing when his leg touched hers. She wasn't supposed to feel this way. It had only ended in misery for her with Trace from the bank. She wasn't going to fall for her new boss. She'd thought it would be easy to close herself off to him since she knew he'd be leaving after Christmas, but this side of him was much more preferable.

The other siblings said a quick hello once the truck dropped them off at the top.

"Walker, right?" Dustin said to Kassidy's second oldest brother. He must have recognized him from high school. They'd never run in the same circles, but the high school wasn't as big as some of the ones in LA.

Walker smiled and stuck his hand out. The two were similarly shaped, although Dustin had about two inches on him.

"Coldwater Creek High. I remember you." Walker stepped back and put his arm around Lauren's shoulder. "This is my wife, Lauren."

Dustin's face scrunched a bit, and it looked like he was trying to think of something. "You have an older brother who graduated the same year as us, right? I can't remember his name right now."

"Preston," Lauren said with a bright smile.

The rest of the gang were all ready to go, but the sleds were few.

Easton walked over and gently took the sled in Walker's hand. "You and Lauren are going to have to ride together."

His gaze lingered another second or two before Walker smiled and gave it to him willingly.

Kassidy knew what they were doing, and she wanted to say something, wanted to get mad at them for trying to play matchmaker when that was not something she needed right now. She just needed a stable career so she could finally move out of her parents' home and have a sense of purpose, to feel like she was finally growing up.

"Kassidy, looks like you and Dustin are sharing the black sled." Easton stepped toward them. "It's kind of the fastest sled, so don't fall out, sis."

She slugged him in the shoulder again, and he grabbed the spot, feigning injury.

After setting the sled on the ground, Kassidy danced around it, not sure whether going in front of or behind Dustin would be ideal.

"I can just wait up here if you want to take this one down," she finally said, waving to it.

"Are you scared of going down with me?" Dustin asked, the corner of his mouth turned upward.

At the word scared, her defenses rose. "I'm sorry, but I've had bigger scares on the backs of rodeo horses. Sleds are nothing but a thrill compared to those."

She hopped into the front of the sled, not sure about his prior sledding experience. If she could control it at all, they wouldn't land in a snowbank.

He slid in behind her, his snow pants riding up and revealing his pant legs.

"Are you ready for this?" he said, his lips so close to her ear that it sent a chill down her back.

"Oh yeah." She grabbed the rope and maneuvered them into line with the others. Six sleds lined up next to each other were bound to end with some interesting turns.

"Go!" one of the twins called out from the other side, and everyone pushed off.

At first, Kassidy and Dustin had a good lead, keeping up with Walker and Lauren. Kassidy almost forgot about who was behind her as the wind raced against her face and they went sailing down the lane.

And then they were hit from the side, and as much as Kassidy tried to steer their sled away from the large jump her brothers had created earlier that morning, they ended up going straight over it.

For a few seconds they were airborne, and Kassidy's stomach jumped. That feeling of falling out of the sky with nothing to hold on to caused her to cry out.

Arms wrapped around her as they came down on the ground, and she landed on top of Dustin before they went rolling down the hill. The wind was knocked out of her in the process, but somehow she'd landed twisted in his arms, staring into those turquoise-blue eyes.

Everything around them at that moment seemed to stand

still, and even when she'd regained her air, it was sucked back out again. Dang, he was cute. And he'd done what he could to protect her from the fall. Not that she hadn't taken notice of his strong arms around her. How did he have time to work out with all his meetings and work?

For a moment, she thought he would kiss her, and then she remembered her siblings were just down the hill. Pushing against the ground, she popped up, hoping her brothers didn't notice the extra pink covering her cheeks.

CHAPTER 13

*N*othing good could come from this.

Dustin wasn't sure why he'd wrapped his hands around Kassidy's middle. Maybe it was because she yelled and his instincts reacted, thinking he could protect her. Now all he'd done was land hard on the ground with his arms around a beautiful woman who he was supposed to be avoiding. She was his employee, after all, and he didn't want history to repeat itself.

Dating wasn't in the cards for him, not after all the betrayals he'd gone through over the years. There was no simple, "Hey, I like you and you like me, so let's date and see where this goes." Most of the time, the women who paid him any attention were only seeing dollar signs when they looked in his direction. That's what happened when he became a billionaire after accepting the position as head of Wakefield Fabrication. Women flocked to him because he had a lot of money and then left when they found something better.

But Kassidy had been different to work with so far. She was sincerely trying to do a good job with this setup. And she'd never done anything to butter him up. In fact, the thing he liked most about her was that she wasn't afraid to speak her mind.

"You guys okay up there?" one of her siblings called out.

Kassidy had scrambled out of his arms and to her feet in no time. "Um, er, thanks for helping me." She brushed off the snow from her pants, most likely trying to avoid eye contact.

"I'm just glad you got us to go over the jump. I figured if we'd hit it at the side, we would've rolled down the rest of the hill."

Kassidy finally cracked a smile. "We pretty much did." She leaned over and held out a hand, pulling him to a standing position. She picked up the sled, but he took it from her.

"I've got this," he said, giving her a small smile.

As she walked a few steps in front of him, his heart thundered in his ears. He'd been able to push off the little attraction he'd felt toward her from the first day they met, but something about her spunk coupled with her nerves around him drew him to her even more. And lying there for what was probably only a few seconds, looking into her milky-brown eyes and smelling her vanilla lotion, caused his thoughts to drift. What would it be like to kiss her?

Shaking it off, he focused on the walk down to the truck. Kissing led to a broken heart, one hundred percent of the time in his case.

A few of the siblings claimed they wanted to take a break, so the rest of the group went back up, getting on their own sleds this time. Dustin already missed the heat of Kassidy sitting next to him, and when he glanced over at her on the other side of one of her brothers, he caught her watching him before she moved her head quickly away.

Something had changed between them, and he wondered if he could be strong enough to make it through the next few weeks before the gala. He wasn't ready for another broken heart for Christmas. Even if she was interested, his life was in LA.

After the sun was high in the sky and the snow wasn't as compact as before, they decided to be done. Dustin hadn't felt excitement like this in quite a while, having wrapped himself up in business deals and management for way too long. Taking time to play like he was a kid again had helped immensely with the things that had been hanging over his head.

"Thanks for the invitation," he said to the group. He'd already stripped the clothes he'd borrowed and folded them up on the tailgate as the rest of them stood around drinking hot chocolate from a thermos.

"Here you go," said an older man with graying sideburns. "I'm David McBride. It's nice to finally meet you."

Dustin made sure to look him in the eye when they shook hands. Every time he met anyone, his grandfather's words to make sure people saw him and recognized him from there on out echoed in his head each time. The thought of missing his grandfather hit home, and all he could do was nod.

"Mom said she's working on supper, so we're on our own for lunch. Should we hit up the sandwich shop?" one of the twins asked.

"I'm game for that," the other one responded. The rest seemed to nod in assent. When a bunch of eyes turned in his direction, Dustin shook his head and waved to them.

"I'm good. Thank you for letting me hang out with your family, but I really need to get back home and get some work done."

"On a Saturday?" Mr. McBride asked, grinning like he knew it was possible to get out of.

"Even on a Saturday. There's a lot going on and a new shift in the company. A lot of moving parts that need more direction and order, and I'm the one to make sure all the cogs fit into place." He smiled and waved, walking back to his car parked down the hill from the truck.

He caught Kassidy's eye for a second before getting into the car and was surprised to see her standing there when he closed the door. He turned the car on and rolled down the windows.

"Are you sure you don't want to come get some food with us? Do you even have food at the mansion?" Kassidy asked, looking past him as if she'd be able to look into his refrigerator from here.

He laughed a bit and nodded. "I have plenty of food at the house, and I have some cooking skills, so I'll be fine. Thanks again for the diversion, and I'll see you Monday."

The concern on her face was pulling at the wall he'd erected to keep things like this out, and he rolled up the window and took off, his wheels skidding along the snow. Not the best choice of vehicle to bring to the mountains in December.

He glanced in the rearview mirror and saw her watching the car pull away, an expression he couldn't read on her face. There were so many emotions running through him right now that spending time with her and her family would only have cemented the fact that he would have a harder time leaving Coldwater Creek after the holiday.

He needed to keep his eye on the prize. Finish off the gala for his grandmother and then get back to LA where he wasn't tempted by a girl with spunk and a gorgeous smile.

CHAPTER 14

The next few days passed quickly, with the frequency of Dustin's virtual meeting schedule only increasing. It was nice to have that form of communication, but it also left him more drained than just having to answer a hundred emails.

"Hello, Stockton," he said to the computer screen, rubbing his forehead again.

The issues that had come up in the overall business had been extreme in the last few days. He thought on more than one occasion that the people beneath him should have figured things out. Instead, they all kept coming to him with problems instead of solutions.

"The big machine went down at the factory in Fort Collins this morning. They've had people there to fix it, but some of the parts are so badly damaged that they don't think they can be repaired."

Dustin pulled up the folder for all the information on the Fort Collins branch, searching for the document for when the machine had been purchased. It was over twenty years old and probably due for an upgrade.

Instead of giving the VP of Operations that information, he paused and then asked, "How long have we had that machine?"

"Uh, I'm not sure." Hesitation and panic were written all over the man's face as Dustin watched him search through files on his desk.

"Go to the shared folder in the company files. This is why we need to get everything digital and in the correct spot." He paused, hearing the chiding tone in his voice. Calming down a bit, he said, "It's in the Fort Collins folder, and it looks like the purchase date was over twenty years ago."

Again he waited, staring at the screen. This had been the problem, and Dustin was just now realizing it. He'd been the one to make things easier on everyone, basically doing parts of their jobs. No wonder he felt like he was chained to the computer at all times.

"Do you think we should upgrade that machine?" Stockton asked, looking more unsure of things than Dustin was comfortable with. The man had been with the company for over ten years and in his current position for three.

"I think that would be a good idea," Dustin said, rubbing at his forehead again. "I'll let you handle all the paperwork for that. I've got a million other things to take care of."

"Okay, sounds good." The man looked as though he was ready to hang up, when Dustin held out his hand to gesture to wait.

"Stockton, you're in the position you're in because you've proven yourself in other ways throughout the years. Show me that leadership potential. Not every decision needs to go through me."

"Sounds good, boss," the man said, his cheeks turning a deep shade of red.

They hung up the call, and Dustin leaned back in his

chair, resting his hands on the back of his head and stretching just a bit.

"At least you were nice-ish about that," a voice called from behind him.

Dustin jumped, surprised that Kassidy was there. "I didn't hear you come in." He usually listened for her in between calls, but she hadn't come at her usual time today.

"I came in through the garage this time. I passed your grandmother on the road up. For an older woman, she definitely gets out a lot." She chuckled, and he joined in for a second. "Thanks for the code, by the way. I had to drop off some of the decorations I've found so far."

Dustin glanced at his phone, surprised to see it was already the eighth of December. "Are you finding everything you need?"

Kassidy laughed, setting a couple of boxes on the table next to him. "Yep. I did have to negotiate with a woman for some of the twinkle lights she had in her cart. She had so much in her cart that I'm betting it will end up stuffed in the closet for five years with no air."

Dustin laughed, surprised at the seriousness of her face. "Speaking from experience?"

"I love my mother, but that is her to a T. My dad built an extra shed out back that was supposed to be one of those she-sheds, like a work area for her? Yeah, it's packed to the rafters with supplies, and my mom hasn't been out there in months."

Dustin smiled, thinking of his own mother. She'd never been into crafting, focusing a lot of time on the charities she ran and helping Dustin with his schoolwork or just hanging out with him. But she'd always loved to paint.

A sudden pang of sadness hit him at the memory of her sitting by the window, painting the scene outside. That had happened so long ago that he was surprised he still remembered.

"Maybe it's kind of a therapy for her?" Dustin offered.

"I've never thought of it like that. Retail therapy to me has always been a clothes-shopping spree, but I can see how craft supplies could do the same thing. She's always excited when one of us kids needs something for a project and she's got it stuffed in there." Kassidy laughed, the slight rumble of it causing Dustin to join in.

"My grandmother is the same way. I think she's been holding on to things we could've gotten rid of decades ago, but then she worries she or someone else will need it soon after she's thrown it out. I'll probably have to hire someone to go through her belongings when she dies. I doubt she's gotten rid of anything that belonged to my grandfather."

He turned his head to glance at the boxes on the table. "What are these?"

She pushed them toward him and opened the top box. "Just a few ornaments."

He gazed inside, seeing several ornaments of different shapes. They were larger than the typical size for most trees, if he didn't count the large glass balls the decorators had always used in the past.

"Did you decide on a theme?" he asked, trying to figure out how these all connected.

"I went with the Twelve Days of Christmas. Some of the ornaments are mixed up between the boxes, like there." She leaned over and pointed to one of the sculptures. "Seven maids a milking in the same box as the four calling birds and partridge in a pear tree."

It took Dustin a minute to recognize a bird in the branches of the tree. "Okay, I think I see it."

"What do you think? Yay or nay?" Kassidy asked him, eyebrow raised with the question.

"Um, I mean, they're cool."

"But?" Kassidy asked, her hand now on her hip.

Dustin studied her face. Would she be willing to hear his honest opinion without flipping out on him?

"I'm just not feeling these. It took me a while to figure out what the figurines were, and the workmanship isn't all that great either."

Kassidy went still, tipping her chin up in the air and nodding. Her eyes flashed just a second before she leaned down and closed up the box. "That's all I needed to know." She lifted the two boxes into her arms and turned to head back out the way she'd come in.

Dustin stood from the chair he'd been sitting in for a few hours already and hobbled a couple of steps until his back straightened from lack of movement. He need to order a real office chair. Sitting in a dining room chair for hours on end for over four weeks was only going to make things worse.

"Kassidy, where are you going?"

She didn't say anything, and he finally caught her arm and turned her around before she walked out the door leading to the garage.

She turned toward him, forcing a smile before she said, "I'm going to return these and figure out a new solution."

That last word caused him to pause. She was the first person in his employ to say that in days. Or ever.

"Do you need help?" he asked, surprising himself. He had reports to file and information to go through for business deals coming up, not to mention the data for the local factory. But all of it sounded like more than he could handle today, and he just needed some kind of a mental break.

"You want to help me?" she asked, looking more surprised than he did. "Don't you have some big decisions to make about a local factory?"

For a moment, he saw vulnerability in her eyes, and he

wondered what that had to do with the factory. "There are always big decisions to be made when you're in my position, but I need to get out of here. Looking at something that doesn't have to do with numbers or money might help relieve the stress building in my head again."

"You get headaches a lot, huh?" Kassidy said, walking out into the garage. There were several large boxes already piled up along the wall, all similar to the ones she'd brought in.

"More so since I came here. Maybe it's the altitude change."

Kassidy went to open the door of her Jeep, when Dustin reached over and touched her hand, the gesture feeling more intimate than he'd planned. Dropping his hand back to his side, he said, "We'll take my ride."

Her gaze slid over the car, and a smile spread across her face. "I've always wanted to ride in one of these."

He helped her load the boxes in the trunk and the backseat, barely having enough room for all of them, and she jumped into the passenger side before he could move to open the door for her. At least his grandmother wasn't there to see it. She'd have berated him up and down for letting a girl help herself into a vehicle.

Once they were in and driving down the hill, Kassidy turned to him and said, "I don't think it's the altitude, Mr. Hotshot Businessman. I think it's the fact that you don't ever rest. I've only seen you out of a suit a handful of times. What you need is a vacation."

"You think my headaches are from stress? I'm the CEO of my company. How am I supposed to get away from stress?"

She grinned, her white teeth shining out against her olive skin and the dark hair framing her face. "Learn to relax when you can relax. Like right now. Do you have to wear a suit while you work from home? No!"

Dustin adjusted his suit jacket. "This is part of the uniform."

Kassidy shook her head. "Not always. I promise your work isn't going to suffer if you're not wearing a tie."

Dustin took the turns quickly, his foot pressing onto the gas pedal, and Kassidy lifted her hand to hold on to the handle above her, her face flushed and eyes wide with terror. "I thought you were used to horses. Why are you flinching?"

She shook her head. "Real horses, not the ones in an engine. And when I'm going fast, I know how to control it and trust myself that I can make the tight turns."

"So you don't trust me?" he said, his smile turning devilish. The sun had melted some of the snow on the road, but it was still slushy, and he finally slowed down a bit. He may have been up and down that road hundreds of times growing up, but he still didn't trust himself completely in the snow since it had been so long since he'd driven in it.

She squirmed, and he could see the white of her knuckles as she gripped the bar. "You almost ran me and Easton over on the sleds, so, no, I don't trust you." The last part came out as a scream as he glanced over and then back, course-correcting away from a ledge.

Kassidy blew out a long breath, and he was sure she was going to hyperventilate.

"Are you okay?" he asked, trying to keep a smile from his face.

"*No*, I'm not okay. You almost ran us off the road. Stop the car. I want to get out."

Dustin slowed the car but didn't stop. "I'm sorry, Kassidy. I was just playing around. I drove this road so many times in my teens that I still do it sometimes while I sleep."

"I prefer to stay alive, thank you very much. I've only lived for twenty-five years and don't have anything set up if I die, so don't be an idiot."

He took the roads more carefully now, enjoying the bright sunshine of the day sparkling off the few leaves resting on top of the snow as they passed.

"What made you want to get into design?" he asked, hoping to break the tense silence.

Kassidy turned, the deep frown line in her forehead visible.

"You want to know more about me?" She jabbed her pointer finger into her chest, her eyebrows nearly reaching her hairline.

"Yeah, what? Am I that unapproachable? You're working with me for the next couple of weeks. We might as well get to know each other a bit." He was more and more curious about her every time she came to the house. From all he'd gathered, she'd been a barrel racer and now wanted to be an event planner. It was kind of a big leap between the two things, but he could understand wanting something different.

The car grew silent for several minutes, and he thought she was going to ignore him completely.

"I've always liked planning things. I recently planned a baby shower for my sister-in-law, and it was the best rush to see how it turned out after it was all set up. You probably already know about it from my application." She turned to him then, her jaw moving up and down a couple of times with no words coming out, like she was trying to figure out what to say. "What made you pick me?"

Dustin grinned and glanced at her for a second before turning back to the road. They'd made it to the bottom of the hill, and he had to inch out enough to see past the small curve that blocked his sight to the right.

"I think it was you telling me off. I figured if you were tough enough to do that, you'd be tough enough to handle whatever was thrown at you. And believe me, returning these ornaments is just the beginning. I'm sure my grand-mother will have plenty of ideas when she's done with all of her errands."

He could see Kassidy gulp out of the corner of his eye and tried to hide his smile this time.

"Are you sure she lives at the mansion?" Kassidy asked, her lips slightly turned up. "Because today was the first time I've seen her near the place, and she was leaving in an SUV."

"The woman is eighty-five and has the energy to rival me sometimes. She still nags like I'm a little kid, though." Dustin shook his head, thinking of all the times she'd dropped hints about wanting great-grandchildren and how he needed to find someone to settle down with. At least she hadn't been around much to do that since he'd arrived.

The more he thought about that, he wondered why she'd even invited him home if she wasn't going to be there much.

"When you drive like that, I can understand why," Kassidy said, laughing.

"I pictured you as the carefree type, up for anything," Dustin said before he could stop himself.

That frown line appeared just above her eyebrows again, and he knew he'd hit a sore spot.

"I know when to play around and when to get serious." She paused, staring out the window like she would see some-thing she needed. "I just feel like I should have things all figured out by now, you know? Like I had all these plans after high school, and I've accomplished some of them, but I just don't know which direction to go."

"Sometimes I wish I had that problem. It would be nice to have a few days here and there with no schedule and to be able to do what I want to do."

"Why not? You're the boss. Can't you arrange your schedule how you want it?" Kassidy said it so simply, like it was just that easy. But from the evidence of his call with

Stockton today, he knew it wasn't going to be that easy. Maybe down the road a ways when he'd broken his employees and himself of the habit of taking over and fixing things on his own.

But right now? The thought of it gave him a headache.

When he didn't respond, still lost in his thoughts of rearranging things, Kassidy asked, "What is it you want to do?"

"I want to ski and surf and be a bum for a little bit." The words were something he'd never consciously thought about, but life right now consisted of spreadsheets and meetings. Doing anything outside would be more exciting than that. Even just the time he'd gone sledding with Kassidy's family had rejuvenated him.

"If only you could do all those in Coldwater Creek," she said thoughtfully. "The ski resort is about twenty minutes north and already open for the season."

"Coldwater Creek has a ski resort?" he asked, surprised by that bit of news. It had always been too small to warrant spending the money, but then again, there had been a lot of new growth in the area since he'd been gone.

"Just go to the turnoff right before Alpine, and you're on your way."

He nodded, maneuvering into town. "Good to know. Where do you need to go?" He gestured to the boxes lying in his backseat.

People walked across the crosswalk, delaying his forward progress.

"To the Christmas shop, over on First East." She leaned her elbow on the console and pointed across him to the shop decked out in all the festivities of the season. When she slid back into her seat, he could smell the vanilla scent he remembered from when he'd caught her on their tumble down the sledding hill.

Walking into the room, the smell of cinnamon pinecones

hit him, just like how his mother loved to decorate things when he was younger. The memory made it hard to breathe, and he pretended to be checking out another aisle as Kassidy talked to the attendant behind the counter. No need to let her or anyone see him tear up when he could do nothing but let the memory wash over him.

A few minutes later, she came back and joined him. He'd found his way to the section with ornaments of varieties from gaudy to classic all along the aisle.

"This place is huge," he said, glancing around the rest of the store. "I didn't realize we basically had a Christmas emporium here."

She laughed and picked up a small ornament. The chime of the bell at the end had a high, tinny sound.

"That's cool," he said, stepping next to her and lifting it from her hands.

The warmth in her fingers moved through him again, and he had to remind himself that touching her, even lightly, needed to be off-limits. He was out shopping with her already, which he never would have dreamed of doing. He didn't need to get his hopes up that he could actually be in a successful relationship when all the others had bombed.

Kassidy nodded. "I love bells. I've always loved the group that carols around playing bells in the white snow. It's like the perfect symbol of Christmas."

"Why choose 'The Twelve Days of Christmas,' then? Why not do something like 'Jingle Bells'?" He studied her face, seeing the emotions of irritation and surprise wash over her.

"Because 'Jingle Bells' isn't all fancy-schmancy, and that's what I need to do to impress your grandmother. And all the other important people you said were coming to the gala." She turned to him, her eyes pleading for some kind of answer.

"My grandma loves Christmas in general. She would love

'The Twelve Days of Christmas' idea, but I think you would much rather go in the direction of bells. She would love something different too." He raised an eyebrow and gave her a cockeyed smile until she grinned and chuckled a bit.

"You're right. It was actually first on my list, but I took it off." She bit the inside of her cheek, her gaze darting down the aisle.

Dustin waved at the selection of bells in front of them. "I think it will work out well. Trust your gut."

"Okay," she began, pulling a few bells off the rack in front of them, sticking them into the small basket she'd picked up. "New plan. I'll just have to transform some of the other ideas I've already planned out, but that won't be too hard. Pivot and move forward."

With the basket nearly filled already, Dustin stepped away and called over his shoulder, "And it looks like we're going to need a cart."

Pivot and move forward. Wise words from the girl who was more interesting to him at the moment than all the business he thought he needed to survive.

CHAPTER 15

This whole day was surreal.

Granted, Dustin probably thought Kassidy had been freaking out when she'd nearly screamed in the car, holding on to the "oh crap" handle with all the strength she had in her, as if that would magically allow her to take over the steering wheel from the passenger seat. But in those moments, flashbacks of an accident she'd been in several years ago took over her vision. The collision had nearly killed one of her good friends, and she hoped to avoid going through that again.

But then he'd been helpful, nice even, when they discussed options for the gala's theme. Why couldn't she just go back to being frustrated with him? Then Kassidy could keep telling herself that a relationship with him was pointless to pursue. Her brain knew it wouldn't work out no matter what, but her heart kept betraying her every time he was around.

The Maserati was packed with boxes and bags, allowing her to feel some measure of comfort. Dustin kept saying she still had over two weeks to pull this off, like that could equal a year's worth of preparation. He didn't get that there was a lot more to do than just buy ornaments. But at least they'd been able to help out Carla, the Christmas shop owner, with more sales than she'd had in the last six months combined.

A few days passed, and she was surprised to get a few texts about random things from Dustin. He tried to be so tough and unreachable, but Kassidy was beginning to think it was his defense to keep people out. What made him afraid of getting hurt?

The two of them had talked here and there throughout the week, but only about basic everyday things, nothing deep or intrusive, which Kassidy appreciated. The last thing she needed was someone to get attached to and then have him leave without a thought of what she wanted.

"Do you want to grab some dinner tonight?" he'd asked that Friday morning.

"Sure. What's the occasion?" It had been a long, long time since a guy had asked her out to dinner, and since they weren't dating, she was more than curious.

He'd chuckled a bit. "You've been working a lot, and you said you needed to get some things from Jackson for the gala. Why not make it a trip together?"

He picked her up a few minutes early, but she'd made sure to be ready and walking up the long driveway to the road when he came by. The cold was worth it to not hear her brother's remarks for the next week about her dating her boss...again.

They were heading up to Jackson in his car, and this time he made sure to drive much safer, keeping his eyes on the road. It eased the anxiety she'd felt the first time around.

Once they walked into the restaurant, she knew she was underdressed in her dark blue jeans and the nicest blouse she owned. If she'd known they would be going to a fancier restaurant, she would have broken out one of her Sunday dresses to bridge that gap even a little.

"What's wrong?" Dustin asked once their food arrived, unrolling the napkin from the silverware and placing it across his lap.

"Um, you're in a suit, as per usual, and I'm looking like I'd be better off at the grill across the street." She jutted her thumb in the direction of the door and let her eyes give him a fair warning of how on edge she felt. "Grab dinner" was like going to a diner or fast food restaurant, definitely not fine dining.

Not only did she feel undressed, but she was also nervous about what dinner might mean. She did need to get a few things from one of the stores she'd ordered from, but in *her* book, friends didn't go to super nice places to eat. The prices weren't even listed on the menu. She'd have to sneak into the bathroom and check her banking account to see if she even had money to pay for this.

Were they supposed to talk about work stuff? Or had he invited her because he was bored again, like when he'd followed her shopping?

"You're fine. It's just nice to have someone with me instead of eating alone."

Well, there was her answer to that question. He didn't think about her more than just a placeholder for his own ego. That was rich. If it weren't another hour to get back to Coldwater Creek, she'd have headed out and found herself a cab or Uber to take her home. The price tag on a nearly forty-mile-ride back was more than she could swing right now.

"I mean, I usually eat out by myself and get looks from people who either pity me for being alone or recognize me and then start whispering, trying to figure out a way to 'casually' come talk to me." He began cutting into his steak, but

Kassidy caught a vulnerability there that she'd never noticed before.

Guilt pricked at her chest. She shouldn't have judged so harshly. With a quick chuckle, she said, "I have no idea how that feels, actually. But it sounds rough."

He smiled, taking a sip from his water glass and setting it down. "I enjoy your company as well, so that helps."

Was that a compliment from Dustin Wakefield? He'd been so blunt about her ornament choice a couple of weeks ago, and she'd waited to hear something similar every time she was with him now. But after several encounters together, she realized it was because he had to speak his mind. Now it was a welcome relief to be around him because she knew what he said was the honest truth, not something to try and make her feel better through false pretenses.

"Thank you. You're not bad yourself, when you pull yourself away from that computer."

He glanced up at her through hooded eyes and smiled, the look causing her stomach to do somersaults.

"This is true. My headaches haven't been quite as bad the past week."

They ate their food in silence, and for some reason, Kassidy felt like she needed to keep the conversation going.

"What are your Christmas traditions?" Why was it when she was talking to him that the most ridiculous things popped out of her mouth? He was Mr. Billionaire. Of course he had things to do and places to go for the holiday.

His eyes got a faraway look, and he smiled for a few seconds before his expression turned to a frown. "I'm not really sure we have any outside the gala. There were things my parents used to do for me, before the accident, and my grandparents tried to keep those alive through the years."

"So, what kind of things?"

He tilted his head to the side, his eyebrow raised as if questioning her motives.

Kassidy raised her hands and said, "I'm not going to sell the information to *Coldwater Creek Gazette*. I just like hearing about people's traditions and thought it might help put a few personal touches to the gala."

He set his fork and knife down before lifting his napkin to wipe around his mouth. Kassidy could see he was trying to come up with something to share. "It's been a while since I've thought of it, but a tradition from my mother's family was to hide a pickle in the tree."

Kassidy tried to keep from laughing, but she had to cover her mouth with her hand for a few seconds while she got things under control. His serious expression told her he'd just shared something deeply personal.

"I'm sorry, a pickle? In a Christmas tree?" She could imagine a wet pickle sitting on a branch, dripping juice all over the ornaments below.

Dustin searched her face, and then something clicked, causing him to laugh. "Not a real pickle. It was a glass one. Whoever found it first got an extra present to open, usually a bag of candy or something small. But since I was the only child, guess who always got it?" He pointed to himself at the same time Kassidy said, "You."

She chuckled. "An only child. That would be different. The house would be much quieter anyway, instead of all my brothers fighting or smelling up every room they enter." She cringed, remembering how she'd actually started scrubbing around their toilet while she waited for word about this job. "So how did the tradition of the pickle start?"

"My mom's family comes from Germany, and I guess it's something they do over there. I never asked for the full details." He shrugged, picking up his silverware again. "What about you? What traditions do the McBrides follow every year?"

Kassidy shook her head, laughing. "I don't even think I could name all of them. I think each person in the family has come up with at least three or four things we have to do in December. And now, with in-laws coming in, it's looking like we'll have to start celebrating on Black Friday to get them all in."

"That many, huh? What's your favorite?" he asked, breaking apart his roll and slicing a small section from the butterball.

"Gingerbread houses. Okay, so they aren't technically gingerbread every year. Sometimes my mom just uses graham crackers when she doesn't have much time, but we get pretty intense. We have judges even."

Dustin laughed, lifting the back of his hand to cover his mouth while he chewed and swallowed. "You have judges for your candy houses?"

"Oh yeah. It's seriously fun." Kassidy saw his excitement, and the next words were out before she had a chance to think. "You should come."

"Decorate a candy Christmas house?" He reached up and tugged at his collar. "I'm more of an analytical guy. Creative is not something people would use to describe me, and if there are judges, I think I might sit that one out."

Shaking her head, Kassidy said, "Not a chance. You haven't celebrated Christmas until you've joined in a McBride family gingerbread-house-making competition."

"That is quite a mouthful."

"But you're coming. You can take a night off from work and enjoy a little Christmas cheer." She smiled, surprised at how much she wanted him to agree. With his suit coat off, she had to avoid glancing down at the button-up shirt pulling against his biceps. Every time she did that, she thought about his arms around her as they tumbled down the sledding hill.

He stared at her, his eyes bluer at the moment, looking like a piece of the night sky. "I think I can make that work."

Now that she thought of it, inviting him was the worst idea she could have proposed. Competition ran strong in the McBride blood, and this was just one of many events to boast about for the entire year after. And her brothers would never let her live it down.

After dinner wrapped up, he drove her over to pick up the three boxes the owner of the boutique store had held for her. Once they headed back to Coldwater Creek, Kassidy tried to keep her thoughts on what she needed to do tomorrow for the gala. Time was a small commodity. But instead, she was replaying the conversations at dinner.

Nothing signaled that this had been a real date. Sure, he'd paid for the meal, but the whole feel had been that it was a business meeting. At least she'd had company on the long drive to Jackson.

But she wanted it to mean something more, wanted it to be the catalyst to a relationship. It would be awesome to think back on tonight as a memory she'd keep forever. And yet, there was still a weird formality between them that she was sure she'd just broken.

He hadn't come to a decision about closing the plant in town either, and she wondered if he did end up closing it down, would she be hurt? Or could she understand it from his point of view?

Focus on the gala. The gala was the key to her future as an event planner, and from there she could figure out where she wanted to be and who she wanted to be with. If he didn't have plans to stay beyond Christmas, she wasn't going to push the issue.

It had been over a week since they'd all gone sledding, and her siblings still kept giving Kassidy guff about the tumble down the hill into Dustin's arms.

To be honest, there weren't many moments in between their comments when she wasn't thinking about it either. It was Monday, and she needed to go to the mansion. If only she knew when Dustin would actually leave the house for something. Then she could sneak in there and get done what she needed without complicating things, like her developing feelings for the CEO.

She'd made a lot of mistakes in her life, and she was determined not to repeat what she'd gone through after dating Trace.

Her Jeep finally made it up the steep incline to the mansion, and once she opened the garage door, her stomach sank as she saw his car parked inside. Did the guy ever leave aside from going to the same places she was?

Then her brain pulled up the time he'd brought her the paper to her house, and when he'd been driving around and joined them sledding.

Tilting her head back, she straightened her shoulders and strode in, hoping she could get what she needed and then head out to finish the ever-growing list of purchases to decorate the mansion.

"I need you to schedule a meeting with Greggerson for either later today or tomorrow. I need the numbers and projections for the beginning of the year." For once, it sounded like he wasn't on a conference call as she didn't hear the person on the other end talking.

She decided to sneak past him, hoping to get into the great room just on the other side of the wall, but she'd have to walk across his line of sight. With how her emotions had been all weekend, analyzing every little thing that had happened between them like a seventeen-year-old with a crush, the best thing was for her to avoid him as much as possible.

A guy as good-looking as he was and with as much money as he had, he could get anyone. She was fooling herself if she thought she could turn his head.

She'd made it two steps past him when he said, "Bye."

Maybe he hadn't seen her.

"Hello, Kassidy. How was your weekend?" The warmth in his voice caused her to turn, and she smiled, playing with the coat she'd taken off and draped over her arm.

"It was good. Just finished some ideas for decorating. How about you?" The words came out strangled, and Kassidy willed herself to go to that place of steel, the one she'd used every time she readied for a race around the barrels.

"Good. I got a lot done here."

They looked at each other for several seconds and then spoke at the same time.

"I'm just going to—"

"Please let me know if—"

"—get some measurements of the—"

"—you need anything." He smiled, and Kassidy stopped mid-sentence, unable to concentrate on the words she'd been about to say as she was caught in the trance of his smile.

"Oh, as far as decorations," he said, standing, "I talked to my grandmother yesterday, and she said there are a ton of old decorations in the storage room."

He waved for her to follow him, and instead of going downstairs, where she assumed most storage rooms were kept, he led her upstairs. She'd never been up in that part of the house, but the hallway seemed to go on and on, with doors on both sides every twenty or so feet as she followed him.

"You don't have to use any of this if it doesn't work with what you've already got planned. I just figured I'd show it to you as an option. I know trying to plan this thing in three weeks can be tricky when trying to get everything shipped here."

Kassidy grunted in agreement. That had been the most time-intensive part of planning. Ordering things was the top priority, and she had to keep crossing her fingers that the items wouldn't be back-ordered, canceled, or delayed.

He opened the door at the end of the hall, revealing a stairway to a massive room with rows and rows of totes, all of them neatly labeled.

"Wow, I don't think I've ever seen an attic this well-organized before." Kassidy walked down the first section, taking in the names of what was in the boxes.

"That's my grandmother. When she and my grandfather first married, he was trying to start this business. She worked with ladies in her neighborhood on organization. I guess by the time things took off with the fabrication company, she'd built her business enough to sell it to someone else."

"So your entire family is full of entrepreneurs, then?" Kassidy said with a smile.

"They definitely had that spirit. I'm just trying to keep it up, to not let down the legacy of what they built all those years ago."

Kassidy folded her arms over her middle. "Is that why you don't ever stop working? You're afraid it will go downhill?"

Dustin's eyebrows cinched together, and the muscle along his jaw flexed for a few seconds before he nodded. "Everyone thinks my life is so glamorous. They just see the few times I step out to an event and think my life is so charmed. What they don't see is the behind-the-scenes to get it to all work."

"I can understand your having to put in a lot of time, but you're the big boss. Don't you have people underneath you who can take some of the responsibility off your plate?"

"My grandfather did whatever he could to help the company grow. If I don't do the same, we'll have to start laying people off."

"Not necessarily," Kassidy said, her stubborn streak beginning to show its colors. "If you think about it, your grandfather had to do a lot of things without the technology we have today. There's got to be some way you can automate parts of your business, or at least have different plans of instructions for different departments so you're not always the go-to man."

He smiled at that. "What makes you think that?"

"You have vice presidents and thousands of other employees underneath you. If everyone took a little part, that would make your life much easier, don't you think?"

From the look on his face, she'd touched a tough spot, so she hurried on, hoping to avoid more awkwardness. "But I'm not the one to tell you how to do your job. I'm just trying to figure out what I want to do with my life as well, so I guess that's just the secret of life we're searching for."

He chuckled at that and then turned to the rows around

him. "Okay, this is baby stuff from my dad. So Christmas will be down the row some more."

Kassidy opened her mouth to remark on how the grandmother had kept things here that she probably hadn't seen in a long time, but then she remembered that Dustin's parents had been killed when he was younger. Death makes people more sentimental than any other event in life. And keeping this stuff was in no way different than what Kassidy's mother kept in her craft shed.

Kassidy followed Dustin and counted thirty-seven boxes of Christmas decor. If it were possible, her eyes would go even wider. "Wow, that is a lot of stuff."

"It's a big place. I'm sure it won't be enough to get what you're planning done. But there are some things that could bring back a little of the nostalgia that a lot of people felt coming here, don't you think?"

Kassidy nodded, excited and overwhelmed at the idea of going through all those boxes. At least it was still early in the day. She'd have to get started now if she wanted to finish before midnight.

"Let me know if you need anything," Dustin said, walking back in the direction of the door.

Kassidy pulled down a box and opened it, finding several old-time lanterns inside. The next one held dozens of matching candles, which would be nice for all the windows. Even though she'd never been to the East Coast, she loved the idea of having a candle shining brightly in each window. And on the front of the mansion alone, there were at least twenty-five.

Time had passed faster than she'd expected when Dustin appeared upstairs again.

"Still going through everything?" he asked, his hands stuffed into the pockets of his slacks. He looked so casual like that, and the slightly mussed state of his hair did something to her stomach, making it flutter like their flight off the sled jump but in a good way.

"Yep. There is so much that looks brand-new. I should be able to use most of it. I just can't believe you have all this up here." She glanced down at her notebook, remembering she needed to write down that there were forty white circular tablecloths in one of the bins.

"Yeah, it's a lot. But it's my grandmother's stuff, so I can't really complain." He said it casually, but Kassidy had to hold on to one of the shelves before she fell over from surprise.

"But there's got to be some stuff of yours in here, right?" She took a few steps down from where all the Christmas boxes were placed on shelves, finding at least six totes with Dustin's name on them. "Bingo," she said, pointing to the section.

He laughed and walked over, opening one of them and closing the lid quickly. "Yeah, let's just leave those alone."

Kassidy closed the distance between them and went to open the lid. Before she got it unlatched, his hand bumped hers away.

She turned to him, giving him a wide smile of surprise. "You're not going to let me look in there?"

"I would think you have dozens of others to go through first." His raised eyebrow was like a challenge, and she used a hip to push him out of the way, opening the box an inch to find several colorful drawings that had been done by a five or six-year-old.

His arms went around her middle, pulling her away from the shelves. He pulled too hard, and they slammed into the shelving unit behind them. Kassidy couldn't help but laugh, and he joined in, his upper body shaking with the effort.

"What do you mean you're not creative? Those had some flair to them," Kassidy said after they'd each calmed down a bit.

"Well, that talent never grew, then." He glanced around at all the boxes. "I don't know what I'll do with all this when I eventually sell the place."

"You're going to sell the mansion?" Kassidy asked, her smile dropping. The last few words had bite to them, as if he'd just told her Christmas was canceled or something.

Even though she'd been lucky enough to get the job this year, she'd daydreamed that she'd be able to decorate the mansion for years to come after she planned this year to a T. But if the owners were moving, she wouldn't have that luxury.

"Hold on. I'm not selling it until my grandmother passes on. She originally wanted to give this to me as a present for my wedding. But since I'm not attached, she's giving it to me for my thirtieth birthday, the week after the gala." He paused, searching her face for something. "But this is her home. Even if I have the title, I wouldn't sell it while she's still living here."

"But what's going to hold you here, especially if you end up closing the plant?" she said, more of a statement than waiting for his answer.

He studied her expression, and she looked away, wiping at a stray tear.

Without her hearing him cross the room, he was next to her, his hands resting lightly on her upper arms. "Hey, you sound more attached to this place than I am, and I grew up here."

"Exactly!" Kassidy said, her head snapping up to look at him. "There is so much to love about this place. It's always been the Wakefield Mansion. To sell it would lose the history behind it."

He shrugged. "I didn't really think about it like that. I mean, this is the first time I've come back in years besides my grandfather's funeral, so what good is an empty house to the valley?"

He seemed to be staring at her, really asking her opinion on the matter.

"Sounds great in theory, but this will always be Wakefield Mansion. And who knows, maybe you'll be able to work yourself out of a job, or at least assign things to people in order to come visit more often." With his hands on her arms, she was getting light-headed.

"Does that mean you'll actually miss me when I leave?" His voice sounded hopeful, and she lifted her gaze to match his.

"A couple weeks ago, my answer would have been adamantly no. But now I think there's a lot of you that could benefit from a yearly trip to the mountains."

They stood there, staring at one another for longer than was usual, and Kassidy was sure someone had sucked all the air out of the room by vacuum.

"I could get behind that idea, if I had something worth visiting." His gaze was soft, and even as all the alarms went off in her head, she couldn't help the shiver that ran through her as he brushed a section of hair behind her ear.

She opened her mouth to respond but stuttered, not knowing whether to focus on those bright blue eyes or his lips or his hands resting gently on her arms.

He seemed to be contemplating the same, his head bending over an inch before the attic door opened.

Kassidy jumped back, the heat of embarrassment coursing through her cheeks.

"Dusty," a woman called out. "We need to go over the final guest list for the gala tonight." The slightly bent woman climbed the stairs and smiled at the two of them. "Ah, Kassidy McBride, you look just like your mother. She used to run around with

Dustin's father." She paused a moment, looking like she was pushing away all the emotions that came with her son's memory. "I'm Grace Wakefield. You can come along and help too. The sooner we have it figured out, the better. People have already started calling to see if we're still having the gala or not."

"Um, I'm not sure I'd be of much help. I really don't know that many people." She bit the inside of her cheek, waiting for the woman to dismiss her.

Instead, Mrs. Wakefield waved her hand and said, "What better time to learn than now? I have a feeling you'll be decorating this place for years to come. Learning all the usual people who come now will be a benefit in the future."

"But I thought Dustin wanted to—"

Mrs. Wakefield raised her hand again and shook her head. "Whatever Dusty does with the house after I go is his choice, but I'm hoping he'll have a reason to stay."

Both of them had said that within the last few minutes, and Kassidy wondered why his grandmother had said it in front of her.

Of course, if Dustin had leaned in all the way for a kiss, Kassidy would've been in heaven. But life wasn't a fairy tale, and no matter how much she could see herself at the mansion, that was a dream she wasn't qualified for.

CHAPTER 17

Sitting across from Kassidy while his grandmother pulled out card after card of people she'd invited to the gala over the years, Dustin kept stealing glances in her direction. She was beautiful and smart, funny, and he was sorry he hadn't been able to kiss her. He was usually so guarded, but when it came to Kassidy, he trusted her in ways he wouldn't have trusted anyone else.

"John Seaberg. I've heard he's in Canada this year for something with family." His grandma set the card to the side in the growing pile of no's. "Lila Birch. Oh."

The mention of the name of the woman who'd betrayed him five years ago caused his blood to boil. He'd found her making out with the drummer of a popular band the event planner had hired to play at the gala. He could still feel the weight of the velvet box in his pocket as he turned and walked from the room.

That was the last time he'd let himself be fooled. Now his dates were just for show, taking out a different girl to every charity ball and auction where he needed to represent the company. But none of them had mattered to him. No woman had gotten to him.

Except Kassidy.

She was staring at him now, curiosity boiling over. When Dustin's grandmother put the card into the no pile, he picked it up and ripped it to pieces.

"She shouldn't be included in the list ever again," he said, his voice sounding foreign.

"I agree." His grandma gave him that pitying look she'd mastered by the time he'd come to live with her. Turning to Kassidy, she reached out and covered the back of Kassidy's hand with her palm. "She is Dustin's ex-girlfriend. Didn't know how good she had it when she messed things up."

Dustin pressed his thumb and forefinger on either side of his nose, near the eye bones. Another headache was starting, and he stood, walking out the door to get some fresh air. The deck boasted a beautiful view of the valley below, but he only saw it for a second, blowing out a breath in the cold air.

The door opened, and Kassidy slipped out, wrapping her coat around her. She said nothing, only taking a place close to him and staring out at the landscape.

"You don't have to tell me I should be over her. I am." He used his hand to emphasize the fact.

Kassidy shrugged. "I'm not one to judge. It's not like my relationships are book-worthy."

Silence settled around them again, but comfortable, like she didn't expect him to say anything. There were so many sides to Kassidy McBride that he never ceased to be amazed. She wasn't bullying him into talking, which he'd thought she would do from her outburst the day he'd interviewed her.

"I was going to propose the night of the gala, five years ago. She was kissing someone else."

"You can't blame yourself for that. It was probably a good thing she did it. Better to break things off then than to go through a messy divorce. A friend of mine had that happen last year. She's a shell of the person she was before because of it." Her slight smile warmed a section of his chest, even though it was probably below freezing out there and he wasn't wearing a coat.

"To be honest, I've never thought of it like that. I've just always thought I wasn't good enough. Most people see me and think my life is perfect, but that feeling of inadequacy to run a billion-dollar corporation only compounded when it trickled to my personal life."

Kassidy reached out and touched his upper arm, an expression of understanding instead of pity boosting his spirits somewhat.

"You'll be fine. Just take it one day at a time. That's what I'm trying to do."

He grinned. "Is it working?"

She burst out laughing. "Not really, but I can pretend."

Their breath puffed out in big white clouds, the moon casting enough light that the snow appeared to be shimmering.

"How's the planning going?"

He watched as she breathed out a sigh. "Going…well. I think with all the stuff upstairs from past years, you saved me at least two days' worth of shopping online. I'll probably still have to go to Jackson or Idaho Falls to do a bulk run of anything I'm missing, but now I won't have to rent a moving trailer to bring it all here." She laughed, and from the scrunch around her eyes, it was the kind that becomes giddy and uncontrollable, usually from being overly tired.

It was fun seeing her like this, not so frustrated or desperate with her life. Then again, he'd had plenty of moments of that throughout the past few weeks.

"Glad I, or my grandmother, that is, could help." He jutted his thumb in the direction of the house. "We probably better get in there. She'll be calling out here soon enough."

Kassidy gave him a quick smile before stepping in front of him and into the house. The fact that she'd come out there to comfort him meant a lot. Maybe he was just used to people taking more than they gave, but if this was a usual thing with her, he could get used to it.

What else could she add to the front yard?

There was less than a week left before the gala on Christmas Eve next Thursday, and she was fairly confident about how everything would go inside. She'd been working to hang the large garland over the mantel and had needed a quick break, stepping outside to try and get some inspiration for what the guests would see first.

The front courtyard looked so bare from where she was. A few trees grew in front of the house but not enough to block the view of the beauty of the mansion.

"What's wrong?" Dustin asked, his tie loosened around his neck as he walked down the steps toward her. Kassidy was several feet into the snow, trying to see what angles would work for what. "I could see you out here pacing when I pulled up. You must be in the zone because you didn't even hear my horn."

The fact that he was watching her caused her chest to constrict in the way she'd always done when she had crushes in high school.

"I just need some more pieces out here, something to draw the eye."

"You could always decorate the large pine tree over there to the left." He pointed in that direction, and she could see the other side of the valley from that side. It could be like some kind of tribute up high in the dark night sky.

"What do you think about doing carriage or sleigh rides around the property?" she asked, walking out of the snow and stomping her boots on the driveway. The land was over ten acres up on the top and another twenty on the ridge below it. She didn't want to worry about anything down there, but a sleigh ride could be fun and something different for that year.

"Trying to go out with a bang on this, right?" He grinned at her, knowing she didn't like it when he talked about selling the property.

"Just trying to add a little flair of fun for the attendees. We saved a lot on the ornaments, and there's got to be a couple of sleighs we can use from around the valley. My family has plenty of horses to pull them."

"I like it. On one condition: that you'll save me a ride with you around the grounds."

She shook her head and laughed. "You drive a hard bargain, but I think I can consent to that."

His nearness caused her heart to pick up speed. She just needed to forget him, finish this event, and move on. That's what he would do.

They walked back inside, and she gathered up her notebooks.

"Where are you going so fast? Don't you need to stay and take pictures of another room or something?" He waved his arms around, his gaze trying to find something to latch on to.

Kassidy raised an eyebrow, trying to gauge what he

meant by that. "Are you feeling a little lonely up here by yourself on a Friday night?"

"Maybe. I feel like I'm the parent when it comes to my grandmother. She and Margritte are gone a lot, and they're so secretive when they get back." He leaned against a doorframe and smiled. "We could watch a movie or something."

"I can't stay tonight. It's the gingerbread competition. Are you still coming?" She tucked the notebooks and small tablet next to her body, waiting for his answer. She couldn't decide if she wanted him to come or not. Sledding with her family had already brought on countless jokes about the two of them. But maybe she could pretend for one night that something could happen in their future.

"How long does it usually take?" Dustin's expression was neutral, meaning still no decision.

Kassidy leaned against the kitchen counter and stared at him. "When was the last time you decorated a gingerbread house?"

Dustin closed one eye and looked up to the ceiling, his lips moving. "Probably fifteen years ago. I got into that too-cool-teenager stage, and my grandmother stopped pushing it."

"Well, that's ridiculous." She paused and smirked. "To be honest, my family is the most competitive of any family I've ever met, in case you couldn't tell from sledding. I think that's why we're all still willing to do it. To see who will win this year."

"Who won last year?" Dustin asked, his voice conveying his disbelief.

"Hunter did. He went for a 'Christmas in the Jungle' look, complete with a mini treehouse. I do have to say it's going to be hard to top that one." Kassidy laughed, and Dustin joined in. "I'm sure we'll have plenty of candy to decorate and eat."

For a heartbeat, Kassidy was sure he was going to say no.

But then he nodded, and she had to hold back a squeal, nodding her head and giving him a quick smile.

"Beats going over reports all night." He straightened and walked over to get his suit jacket off the back of his chair.

"Wait, there's one rule when it comes to the decorating."

Dustin paused, his jacket dangling over his head as he waited. "A rule to decorating a gingerbread house? Of course, I should've guessed that would happen with you."

"You can't come—or I should say, shouldn't come—in your nice clothes."

He glanced down at his typical slacks, button-up shirt, and tie. "I can't just wear this?"

"I know you probably just walk out of the shower wearing a suit and tie, but my family is a bit more casual than that. And if a food fight breaks out, I don't want to be responsible for replacing…that," she said, waving her hand up and down in front of him, gesturing toward the clothes. "Do you own sweats or jeans or anything like that?"

He slowly replaced his jacket and retained a shocked expression while he walked past her. "There won't be any more strange rules when we get there? Something you've kept hidden?" he said, doubt in his voice.

"I promise I'm doing this for your own good. Food fights aren't unheard of during this thing."

He laughed as he disappeared up the stairs and down the hall. For a moment, she wondered which of the rooms she'd passed on her way to the attic was his. And then she brushed that off. That was too intimate, and she was already slipping against the onslaught of feelings over this guy who just kept surprising her.

She'd seen him as the evil emperor when he'd first arrived, and now he was just a guy who worked too much and didn't know what to do with his money or who to trust completely.

When he came down looking like a model for one of the athletic-gear lines, Kassidy had to look away quickly before she started drooling.

He's just going to leave in a couple of weeks, she kept trying to tell herself. She headed over to the garage door.

"Do you want me to drive?" he asked, shutting the door behind them.

"Maybe just follow me down? Then we don't have to come back for my car."

That was a good answer. Give space between the two of them. She shouldn't have invited him to come tonight in the first place if she wanted a full separation. But it would be so lonely and creepy to stay in the mansion all by himself, and she could semi-dream that something might happen between them. Maybe it wouldn't feel so awkward with Easton and Walker and their wives if Kassidy had someone with her tonight. Not awkward, just envy-provoking.

"Okay, yeah. Probably a good idea."

Giddiness flowed through her as they descended the hill and onto the main road back in the direction of the main part of town. It was like she'd never grown up. She loved this time of year, and the gingerbread contest was one of her absolute favorite traditions.

As she parked the car in her usual spot in the driveway, Dustin pulled up right behind her, turning off the lights and stepping out of the car. His hair was still mussed, and as he came closer, she wondered what it would be like to kiss him. They'd been so close a few days before, but there hadn't really been a chance again.

"You made it," her mom said, standing on the porch wiping her hands off on a dishtowel. "We weren't sure whether you were going to be done with work. Oh, Dustin. We're so happy to have you here."

"I'm happy to be here, Mrs. McBride."

"Tonya, please."

Kassidy smiled. Her family was getting more familiar with him. Would this end up being like her crush on Steve Johnson during her junior year of high school? A lot of hoping with nothing to show for it later?

Next stop: Heartbreak Canyon.

The inside of the McBride home was simple but well-kept, the details of the ranch house looking like they'd been carefully selected. In the kitchen, Dustin's mouth dropped open, surprised by the number of candy bowls on the counter. Small houses were already erected on the plates all around the large island. From the looks of it, the counter was bigger than the one at the mansion. With six children, it had probably been a necessity.

"Hey! It's Dustin," Easton said, shaking Dustin's hand and pulling him in for a quick hug. He'd never been in a place where the people had welcomed him as easily as this. One part of him wondered if they were trying to work some kind of angle, and the other made him think that maybe this was just how they were.

"Back for more crazy?" Hunter asked, throwing a peanut into his mouth.

Tonya slapped his hand lightly as she passed around the side of the island. "Stop telling people we're crazy. As far as they know, we're a nice, normal family." She grinned in Dustin's direction, and he laughed.

Something about this made him feel more at home than he did even in LA.

Kassidy looked at him. "Crazy about sums us up," she said, laughing.

Mr. McBride walked over to him, grinning as he snuck a piece of candy from one of the bowls. "Good to see you again, Dustin." He held his hand out and Dustin reached over to shake it. "You've come to one of the best activities the McBride clan participates in every year."

"Dad," Kassidy said, her eyes growing wide. "That's a bit much, don't you think?"

"David, stop eating the candy," Mrs. McBride said, swatting at her husband's hand as he tried to grab a small handful.

A woman walked into the room, heavily pregnant. Easton strolled toward her and kissed her, rubbing her stomach. "How are my wife and my baby doing?"

"We're good. Just surviving these last few weeks." She turned and walked up to the counter. "Oh, hello. I'm Natalie McBride, Easton's wife. I heard you took quite a spill with Kassidy the other day."

Dustin nodded, glancing at Kassidy, who'd busied herself helping her mother spread out the candy bowls along the counter. "Yeah, but it was fun. I can't believe I've never been down that hill until now."

"We like to keep it a secret," Hunter's twin said, leaning over the counter and sneaking a couple of pretzels.

"Colter," Tonya began, "did you not get enough to eat at dinner? I don't know how we've survived in this house with you boys. You've all got hollow legs."

Colter leaned in for a piece of the licorice, and she blocked him with a wooden spoon. "Go cook yourself some soup or something if you're still hungry."

Dustin laughed, but it waned quickly as he wondered what his life would've been like with siblings. There had been many advantages to being an only child, but having someone to play with and hang out with later in life would've been better than hiding out in the mansion by himself.

Kassidy leaned into Dustin a bit and whispered, "That's my youngest sister, Molly. She's a senior, and she's had a crush on her best friend since, well, forever."

"Is that the guy standing next to her?" Dustin asked, only glancing over for a few seconds before focusing on Kassidy again. She fit in so well with her family, and a little pang of jealousy hit him. So this was what Christmas with a big family felt like.

"Okay, Dad," Tonya said in a loud voice, trying to get everyone's attention over the talking voices and the noise of the television. "Let's get this started."

The group crowded around the counter, and Dustin couldn't believe how many people were in that one room.

"Okay, since Molly and Kassidy brought *special* friends over tonight," Mr. McBride began, his emphasis on special, causing laughter to bubble up from Dustin.

"Dad, really?" Molly and Kassidy both said together.

"We're going to do this in pairs. Sorry, boys, maybe next year you'll bring a girlfriend. We'll accept a fiancée or a wife too. For now, you'll have to partner up." Their dad's smile was devilish, and Dustin felt like he was in some kind of movie because families just didn't interact like this. Then again, he'd basically been raised by his grandparents who'd grown up in a different era, mostly formality with a little fun.

"We'll give you sixty minutes to complete your design. Remember, we're looking based on creativity and..." He turned to his wife and asked, "What were the other things?"

"Really, Dad? All we have to do is slide you some extra licorice and our score goes up," one of the twins said.

Feigning anger, Mr. McBride said, "Go!" He pushed the

button on the oven that began counting down the time. Hands reached in and grabbed several bowls, and the groups dispersed to the tables set up in the corner, except for Molly and the young kid with her, who stood at the other end of the counter. Kassidy set up their house on the island counter where they'd been leaning for most of the bantering session.

"Okay, are you ready for this?" Kassidy asked, rubbing her hands together.

"You weren't kidding when you said it's a competition." He could be as competitive as the rest of them, and he turned to her for direction. "Any ideas on what we should do?"

"What about a rustic cabin with some wonderland scene out front?"

Dustin looked down at the small section of cardboard for them to decorate. "You think we can get all that onto this small square?" he asked, pointing it out.

"Yep. That's plenty of space." She turned to look at the bowls along the counter. "Will you grab the stick pretzels, the powdered sugar, and the gumdrops?" She was already pulling bowls over toward their small house.

Taking a large scoop of the thick frosting, she slathered it onto the side of the house by the time he came back with the requested items.

"You're not starting with the roof?" he asked, setting the bowls down.

"That goes on last. Otherwise, it ends up being bumped a hundred times. Okay, start sticking those pretzel pieces into the side here." She pointed to the section she'd just frosted as she worked on the next side.

Dustin did as he was told, and it was nice to not be the one ordering people around for a minute. As he placed them one on top of another, he was surprised to see that it was looking like a cabin in the woods, the pretzels forming the logs.

"I've never thought of doing it like that."

"Let me guess, you did the Necco roof and then added a few gummy trees around the exterior?" She chuckled, turning her focus back to the house.

Dustin laughed as he recalled the few times he'd done this, her description matching his creations perfectly.

In between adding pieces of candy and bits of coconut to wherever Kassidy instructed, Dustin watched her, taking in the movements of her lips, the concentration she paid to the house, and he felt attraction grow within him. After being around her and her family, how was he going to be able to go back to LA and pretend like his life before had been meaningful?

Kassidy had been right when she'd talked about using the people already underneath him. He needed to stop being the solution for these people and have them come up with their own, instead of allowing them to bring him problems day in and day out.

Could he have a life like this? One with family and laughter, with banter and people who would be there through the hard times?

He'd been working solo for so long that the thought of teamwork did something to help ease that stress.

Mr. McBride began counting down once the timer reached five minutes, breaking away from the football game he was engrossed in long enough to announce it. Mrs. McBride made sure to keep things filled up, seeming to enjoy this as much as the kids did.

Kassidy was busy finally getting to the roof, adding fruity candy in neat rows, when Dustin looked up and said, "Thank you."

She paused, looking at him startled. "For what?"

"For inviting me here." He thought about expounding, but he left it at that. There were so many emotions running through him that he wasn't sure he'd know how to put it all into words.

She grinned, her whole face lighting up as she concentrated again on the roof.

"Ten, nine, eight," her dad called out.

"Grab candy and start pushing it into the frosting," she said, giving a little squeal as she moved along the roofline.

"Three, two, one! Hands up and step away. The judges will come around and check out your creations and then deliberate to decide the winner." Mr. McBride's grin looked like he loved this role.

As her parents started at the other end of the room, Dustin stared down at their creation. "Wow, this looks like it should be entered for some kind of town competition, don't you think?"

Kassidy chuckled, checking on her parents before she adjusted one of the candies on the roof. "I don't know about that, but it was fun. What do you think?"

"I have to say that I doubted you on creating a whole scene in such a small space, but it looks like you're an expert in dealing with miniature ornaments and sculptures."

Kassidy laughed out loud, covering her mouth with her hand as her eyes went wide. "I don't think I'd call what I cut out of the marshmallow a sculpture."

"Well, then, what would you call it?" he asked, laughing. The warmth in the room must have affected the poor marshmallow snowman because it was starting to melt.

Kassidy laughed again and shrugged. "We'll have to see what the judges say."

Her parents had stepped over to the house that Molly and her boyfriend had made, a little bit of laughter coming from them over the decoration of the chimney, which ended up being almost as tall as the house.

Kassidy leaned forward against the counter, her

shoulder touching Dustin's. She didn't seem to notice, so intent to hear what the judges were talking about that he was able to observe her without restraint. The dark brown hair she'd just pulled down from a ponytail cascaded over her shoulders. Her brown eyes seemed alight with mischief, and she giggled, causing her hair to tickle the back of his hand.

She was beautiful, and yet, he loved that her personality had its own quirks to it. He'd met too many women trying to act and be perfect for him that the presence of someone who could speak her mind and wasn't trying to put on airs in front of him was a welcome change.

Why did he have to meet her here? Now? Living here wasn't his permanent plan. He still had the decision of whether to close the factory, and from her previous questions, he knew it would affect her just as much as the others in town.

"The winner is," her dad said, pausing to make sure everyone was listening, "Walker and Lauren. Runner-up goes to Kassidy and Dustin."

She turned to him with a bright face, her mouth open in delight. In a quick moment, she leaned forward, wrapping her arms around his shoulders. By the time he recovered enough to react, she'd already pulled back, embarrassment written all over her face.

"Congrats, man," one of the twins said, holding his hand out to shake.

"Thanks," Dustin said. "I'm going to claim beginner's luck on my part."

"Well, Kassidy's got a lot of talent in the creative areas. It's just taken her a long time to figure that out." The twin winked in Kassidy's direction, and she punched him in the shoulder.

The other one approached and said, "We've heard a few

things floating around town. Are you planning to close the Wakefield factory here in town?"

Everyone within a ten-foot radius went silent, their gaze turning to him. It had been a while since he'd had so many people staring at him like this.

"I haven't made that decision yet, but with the lower production numbers, they do need to demonstrate why it would be valuable to keep them around. I had to push out a meeting I'd scheduled with the managers of the plant from last week to this coming week. My goal is to have everything worked out by Christmas."

Kassidy stiffened next to him, and without looking at her, he knew she disapproved of this just as much as his intention to sell the mansion.

"Numbers don't always explain the whole story," was all she said quietly.

Dustin nodded. "I get that. It's why I'll be working from the plant next week. To make sure I make the right decision."

The conversation drifted to lighter topics, but the tightness in Kassidy never eased up. Dustin finally said good night, part of him frustrated at her reaction. This was his job, to analyze the areas that needed help and to act on the solutions that made sense.

Things were going to shake up a lot once he visited the fabrication plant on Monday. Based on his information, things weren't looking good to keep the plant around. Even layoffs and downsizing didn't seem like the right answer, especially this close to Christmas.

As he took the curves up to the mansion, he knew his loyalty was first to the company—his heart had to settle for second.

How could a body hold so much water? Kassidy felt like she'd been crying all weekend. She'd never cried that much, not even after taking third at Nationals for barrel racing. But the analytical way Dustin had said he might close the fabrication plant stirred up all kinds of worries for her. She'd been nervous about it after her aunt's discussion at Natalie's baby shower, and even when she'd pressed him on it during the interview. Now that it was an actual possibility, she felt sick about what could happen to the town.

Visions that popped up in her mind as she strung lights around the trees outside the mansion on Monday scared her, as if a bomb were on a timer and when it exploded, it would take out the whole town. That was a stretch, but she loved the life she had. Yet, as much as she tried not to, she would probably cry even more once Dustin headed back to California.

He'd been upfront with her about it, but she'd managed to push it to the side with all the excitement of planning the gala. For the first time, she was catching a glimpse of how her future could be here in the valley, planning events and enjoying dinners and holidays with her family so close. But if the plant closed and most of the town had to leave the valley, she would have to go also. She hadn't even made it four months in the city. How would she survive the rest of her life there?

A limo drove up the way, the driver in uniform and the windows tinted. She hadn't seen anyone up at the house besides the people who lived there. Curiosity niggled at her, but this wasn't her life. She was just there to make it look pretty.

Maybe she should get back into training and barrel racing once the new year began. As chaotic as driving around the country was, there was always a fixed destination for the next rodeo.

She finished up a string of Christmas lights and paused a moment, trying to decide if she should pretend to be working to see who was in the car or just head inside to get the next strand. But she had no claim to Dustin no matter who showed up at the Wakefield Mansion, and that longing for him was like trying to hold water in her hands.

They were from two different worlds, and as much disappointment as she'd felt when he didn't kiss her, she knew it was a blessing in disguise. Trying to get over someone like Dustin Wakefield would be a hard feat if she'd fallen all the way in love.

Kassidy walked into the garage, wiping at the halo of hair that managed to slip out of her ponytail as she worked. She didn't bother to fix it, knowing she only had a few hours to decorate before Dustin came home from the factory, and she was determined not to be there. She knew that in his mind, business was business, but for a small town like Coldwater Creek, would he shut it down knowing the town might die?

The frigid air had seeped through her gloves, and now

that they were off, she had to rub her hands together to get some feeling back into them. She rushed to unwind one of the strands of lights, knowing she should do it while next to the tree to avoid tangling, but she wasn't thinking quite right at the moment.

Taking the half-undone strand and three more, she dropped them beside the next tree in the row. She lifted the ladder and moved it underneath where she needed to apply lights, doing her best to keep to herself when the door to the limo was opened by the driver.

Out stepped a woman who looked as though she'd just stepped from a runway, her blowout perfect, makeup flawless, and her clothes top of the line.

Kassidy felt the floppy bun on top of her head again and glanced down at the paint-splattered jeans she'd donned that morning. She obviously hadn't learned that those things brought everyone she didn't want to see around her when she wore them.

The woman took off her sunglasses and glanced around the mansion. When her eyes connected with Kassidy's, she smiled. "Hi, I'm Sage Cutler. Is Dustin here, by chance?"

Kassidy shook her head, not sure what to make of this whole situation. At least the woman hadn't said her name was Lila Birch. "No, he's working at the plant just north of town."

"Know when he'll be back?" the woman asked, rubbing her lips together, evening out the shininess of the dark red lip color.

Kassidy shrugged. "I'm just the event planner." She turned her focus back to the lights, wrapping the end around one of the large branches and methodically wrapping the rest of it around the tree.

"Oh, for the Christmas gala? I've heard so much about that. A bunch of my friends have been in years past, and they said the Wakefields know how to throw a party." Sage bounced a bit in her heels, and Kassidy recognized the nervous energy. The woman was probably waiting for her to respond.

"Yeah, I grew up hearing about them. It's pretty cool that I'm the one putting all the details together." Kassidy paused, stepping down from the ladder. Questions churned through her mind, and the one she wanted the answer to most was on the tip of her tongue before she could stop. "How do you know Dustin?"

No jealousy there. Okay, maybe a little.

"He took me to a charity event about six months ago. We've hung out a couple of times, but I thought I'd come and say hi since I was so close to here for work."

Kassidy's heart sank even further. He'd dated this girl. Yep, no chances left for Kassidy. He was a town killer and a heart breaker.

Unable to hold her tongue, Kassidy said, "I'm not sure what you do, but there is not much work here besides raising cattle and milking cows."

The woman's face turned rosy. "True. I was actually hoping to get an invitation to the gala. I've heard that it's just spectacular, and, well, I'd love to see what it's like, you know?"

Kassidy just nodded, climbing the ladder with the next strand of lights. "I think Dustin's grandmother is inside. You can go ask her about an invitation."

"Thank you. And I'm sure this is going to look amazing." Sage pointed to the trees as she turned to walk inside.

If only the woman had been rude and impolite, Kassidy could've disliked her. But Sage seemed more like her in a way, someone who'd started with humble beginnings but somehow managed to now travel in a limo.

The sun's rays were barely giving off any light, and

Kassidy finished up what she could before cleaning her mess of plastic wrap and cardboard pieces. She didn't want to chance seeing Dustin, knowing that his decision about the plant would impact her life in more ways than one. And if he didn't have the same feelings she did, it was better to just cut bait now, as her father would say.

"It was so nice to meet you, Sage," she heard Grace Wakefield's voice say from the great room. "I hope you have a nice drive to your next job."

Kassidy put several things away in the totes she'd gotten them out of and stored the totes in the spare bedroom on the main floor. When she put on her coat and grabbed her purse, the sound of someone calling her name startled her.

"Kassidy?" Grace called. If Kassidy hadn't seen her sitting in her recliner before, she might have thought a ghost had begun haunting the mansion.

She strode over to stand in front of the older woman, smiling as she took in the comfort of the woman relaxing in her favorite chair. Margritte wasn't hovering around, and Kassidy couldn't hear anything in the kitchen.

"What can I do for you, ma'am?"

The woman grinned and waved her hand in the air. "No ma'am needed here, girl. Margritte had to go into town to get me a few extra pills I've run out of. Would you mind staying here until Dusty comes home?"

All the air in Kassidy's lungs disappeared. She'd thought she was in the clear, that she wouldn't have to see him until maybe the night of the gala and then never again after that.

"Um, sure." Kassidy took off her coat and placed her purse next to her as she sank into the matching recliner across the room. How was she going to get out of this? She glanced up at the television, surprised to see it playing one of those chef reality shows.

"I just love watching all the food they create," Grace said.

She must have seen Kassidy's glance at the screen. "Some of the techniques they use I've never even heard of."

Kassidy laughed at the confusion on the woman's face as the chef talked about coddling her eggs. She'd never heard of such a thing either, and an ease settled over her. She liked this woman. Grace Wakefield might have a lot of money, but she was just as normal as Kassidy's grandmother.

"Those do look delicious," Kassidy said, staring at the screen. "I doubt my meringues would look edible. I'd probably forget and char the top."

Grace laughed, slapping her knee at the same time. "Me too. Then again, it's been so long since I've cooked anything that I might forget to turn off the oven at the end and burn the house down."

"What are you two giggling about in here?" Dustin's voice caused Kassidy to jump nearly out of the seat. She hadn't heard him come in.

"Just mishaps in cooking. How did it go at the plant today, Dusty?" Grace asked, reaching her hand out for him. He stepped closer and leaned down enough for her to kiss his cheek. When he stood, his eyes locked onto Kassidy's.

"I'm still not sure yet, but we'll see what they show me tomorrow."

Kassidy's insides twisted, the hope and fear both twisting around herself, it that were possible.

His grandmother leaned in closer, sniffing the air around him. "Why do you smell like exhaust?"

He shrugged, undoing his tie altogether.

Before he could continue speaking, Kassidy stood, grabbing her coat and purse. "Well, I need to get home and finish up some of the projects we need for this gala to be a hit. Have a good night!" She practically ran out of the house, her heart pumping as though she'd just spurred her favorite horse and had to beat the leader's time around the barrels.

Three days until the gala. If she calculated it all right and got a little help from her family, she might just be able to pull this off.

As long as she came out of it with her heart intact, she would call that a double-win.

CHAPTER 21

"What were you doing at the plant?" Dustin's grandmother asked again.

His thoughts had gone out the door with Kassidy. She'd been so standoffish, and he wished he could change things, get them to go back to how they'd been before her brothers asked about the plant.

The biggest confusion of all was why it bothered her so much. It didn't seem like much of her family worked there since most of them worked on the family ranch.

Shaking his head, he came back to the present. "I worked on one of the machines today." He rubbed at his shoulder with one hand, hoping there was some pain medicine in the cabinet for him to take. He was going to be sore tomorrow.

"You worked on the machines?" His grandmother's tone conveyed disbelief, and he chuckled, slumping down in the chair Kassidy had vacated only a few minutes before. It still smelled like her, vanilla mixed with a cinnamon-type scent.

He nodded. "Yeah, I figured it was the least I could do to understand where they were coming from."

"And? What did you find out?" The mischief in her eyes as she waited for his answer only made him smile wider.

He thought back through the day, to the meetings he'd had with the managers. A few hours had passed before he started to understand what they were trying to explain.

"They construct some of the bigger pieces needed for our equipment. I've always thought we could just outsource it to another factory, but there are some flaws in the system." He paused, enthusiasm pouring through him that he'd finally found the answer to what the numbers weren't telling him. If only Kassidy had stuck around long enough to hear it.

"The machine I worked on absolutely needs two people to work efficiently. It turns out that the HR representative had declined several requests to hire new people, meaning our employees on those machines were taking double the time to finish each piece. Once we hire several other people, production will pick up again and the plant should be just fine."

"And the HR rep?" his grandmother asked.

"Packing his bags and filing for unemployment." That was the part that had irritated him the most. After going through a few things over the past couple of days, and then getting confirmation from the different department managers, it seemed the man would only hire from a temp agency because he got a cut of the fee. The guy had put so many lives at risk because of his greed.

But then again, was that how Kassidy looked at Dustin? That he could jeopardize so many people's lives just for the bottom line?

"She's a special one, isn't she?" His grandmother's voice stirred him out of his thoughts.

"Who?" Had he missed a whole conversation already?

"Kassidy. She was trying to avoid you; I just know it. What did you do this time?" There was the parental tone of his grandmother, chastising him for things he'd messed up on.

Dustin swallowed, thinking about all that had happened in the few weeks since he'd come to Coldwater Creek. He never would've thought he could change in such a short amount of time, but he was beginning to see the importance of getting out from behind the desk and letting others handle the busywork. He needed to be the face of the company and figure out these kinds of problems before they festered to this point.

"I was blunt, as usual. I told her family we weren't sure about keeping the plant open, and now she's not really talking to me." He turned to his grandmother, sitting forward in the recliner, elbows on his knees. "Why would she care about the plant?"

His grandmother got that small smile she did when she was about to reveal some great life lesson. He might not have appreciated it growing up, but he would take whatever she was going to share tonight.

"Dusty, you've had a life sheltered from the pains of needing to look for work, of having shelter and a way to provide for a family. That plant is our flagship, the very first building we started in and worked with our sweat and tears, and sometimes even some blood, to get it running. This town relies on the jobs it provides. Kassidy isn't going to stick around here forever if there isn't a way to provide for herself. Maybe that's the hardest part about it. The unknown."

Dustin mulled that over for a few minutes as his grandmother became engrossed in a show about cupcakes.

"Do you think it could work?" he murmured, not expecting a response.

"What, dear?"

"Kassidy and me. In a relationship. I mean, do you think it could be something that lasts? Or am I just being blind again?" If this wasn't the way to make him feel like he was still in elementary school, then he wasn't sure what would. He may as well pass the girl a note and ask her to check yes or no on whether she wanted to be his girlfriend or not.

His grandmother's grin stretched from ear to ear. "If you're going to ask if she's anything like the girls you usually go for, the answer is no. Has she ever tried to get you before a camera, hoping to get into the papers? She hasn't kissed a drummer…"

Dustin sat up, surprised that she knew about that. He'd never come out and admitted his ex-girlfriend had done that. "How—"

She raised her hand. "Don't ask. What I'm trying to say is, I might not have been around much lately, but I've seen the way that girl looks at you. You'd be lucky to have someone like that by your side."

But could he get her to forgive him? Only time would tell.

CHAPTER 22

It was the day of the gala, and Kassidy was doing her best to breathe. Her family had been there to help her decorate the night before, a few of them staying well past midnight. She'd felt bad that she would be disturbing Dustin and his grandmother, but the woman said Dustin had headed back to LA and that when she took out her hearing aids, she didn't hear much of anything anyway.

Kassidy tried to keep positive, telling herself that him leaving was probably for the best, even though it felt like he'd left a hole in her heart. If he'd already gone, he must've made a decision about the plant. But then again, couldn't he wait two days to go home until after Christmas? And anyway, wasn't he hosting the gala?

Kassidy was putting the finishing touches on everything she'd worked on for the past three weeks, hoping that by staying busy, the loneliness pressing against her chest would ease up a bit. Mostly, she just needed to forget about Dustin Wakefield. He'd gone back to LA early, and she would probably never see him again.

After a few minor mishaps that she'd been able to

straighten out, Kassidy hurried to change and get ready in the guest bedroom on the first floor. She opened a bag and pulled out the dress that her mother had bought for her as an early Christmas present. It was a deep red and fairly simple, with a belt along the waistline and the dress falling to her ankles. At least she wouldn't be uncomfortable as she directed the traffic of the caterers and guests throughout the house.

Hair curled and heels on, she grabbed her notebook and walked out, checking off different parts of her checklist.

"Kassidy, dear?" Grace called out to her. She was dressed in silver sparkles, and Kassidy couldn't help but smile.

"Yes, Grace. What do you need?"

"I think I heard something crash outside. It wasn't one of the sleighs, was it? That would be so sad. Bringing the sleighs in was such a great idea. Would you go check for me, darling?" The woman patted Kassidy's hand and batted her eyelashes at her a few times.

Kassidy glanced up at the clock. Still forty-five minutes until guests were supposed to arrive, and her checklist would take all of that time, if not more. But she couldn't say no to her now.

"Of course. I'll just go out really fast."

She turned to walk toward the front door, when Grace called out, "You'll catch your death in that cold. Grab your coat!"

Slipping the coat on, she shuffled out to where the sleighs were parked, being careful that she didn't trip in the fresh powder that had fallen the night before and into the afternoon.

It only took a moment to scan the area and see that everything was all right. The sleighs and horses were being readied for the night's entertainment. The man on the first sleigh was focused on hooking up his horse to it, and Kassidy decided it would be better to ask now if he'd heard anything rather than to have to come back out again on Grace's request.

"Is everything okay out here?" she asked him, tapping on his shoulder.

The man didn't turn around, only continued with his task. "Yes, should be ready for a ride in about a minute." The voice was gruff, but there was something about it that sounded familiar. But Dustin had already flown back to California, so she dismissed that thought.

"All the others are in line then too?" Kassidy asked, wanting to make sure she could give a full report once she got back inside.

"Will you sit in the sleigh? It will help me adjust this." The man pointed toward the seat in the sleigh.

Kassidy didn't have time for this. "I really need to be going inside. There's still a lot to check on, and I need to make sure the caterers are all set up. I can send someone out to help you." Hunter and Colter should've been there to help by now, but bringing a trailer full of horses up the hill would be a chore in itself.

The man finally glanced up at her and said, "Are you Kassidy McBride?"

"Yes," she responded, wondering how he knew.

"I'm supposed to give you the first ride, as per the request of Mrs. Grace Wakefield."

Kassidy pointed toward the house. "That sounds great and all, but you see, this is a very big party, and I'm kind of the organizer."

The man only gestured to the bench. "Mrs. Wakefield said she would take care of any problems while you're gone."

Thinking of the older woman, Kassidy knew she couldn't say no to the feisty woman. That's why she was out here in the first place. She took the man's gloved hand and slipped into the seat, pulling up the blanket to avoid the chill that filtered straight through her dress.

The man finished what he was doing and walked away, leaving her to wonder what was going on. She dug out her phone and tried to do a mental checklist, just hoping the night didn't get all screwed up by her taking a few extra minutes outside. She hoped the ride only entailed a trip around the parking circle.

"Are you ready for the first ride?" Dustin asked, leaning over the side of the sleigh and catching her off guard. His handsome features reflected the moonlight.

Her heart jolted at his unexpected closeness, and her knees trembled as she looked up at him. Irritation swiftly followed. She frowned. "If this is your idea, I have a lot to do before the guests arrive." Throwing off the blanket, she tried to get out of the sleigh, but he'd hurried around the backside and stood next to the opening.

"Please, Kassidy. Just let me have one trip around the house. You promised, remember?"

If only she could go back and undo that promise. She clicked on her phone to see the time. "Okay, but you have exactly ten minutes before I have to be back in the house ready to receive your guests."

He slid in next to her, his legs touching hers on the slim bench. Picking up the reins, he guided the sleigh onto the path they'd designated for the party. The moon was bright, shining over the snow, making it look like they were in some kind of movie.

"You know this is important to me, to my future. Are you trying to sabotage that too, just like the fabrication plant?" she snapped. She'd tried to let it go, but the pressure of not being in control of what was going on inside with the party setup was getting to her.

"Kassidy, this will only take a minute. I promise that everything is on track for a great night."

She closed her eyes and tried to breathe normally, wishing the nearness of him wouldn't cause her insides to go crazy. Traitorous heart.

"Why did you come back?" she finally said.

He turned to look at her, one eyebrow raised in confusion. "To Coldwater Creek? Originally because of my grandmother, but I'm hoping I have another reason to be here."

"You didn't fly to California?" She paused a moment and said, "Your grandmother said you had to go back."

"I've been in meetings all day but I haven't left Coldwater Creek." He turned to glance at her before guiding the horses through the woods at the side of the property. "I'm not closing down the plant."

"Wait, what?"

"When I went there on Monday, I found out the real cause of the problem. They were understaffed. Things will be fixed there after Christmas, when they'll be hiring several new people to operate the machines. And, at the request of several employees, we'll be implementing an onsite daycare and preschool. Hopefully, that will ease some of the worries about trying to find childcare."

A weight lifted from Kassidy's shoulders that she hadn't realized she'd been carrying around. If the plant wasn't going to close, then her future wasn't as shaky as she'd thought. And the fact that he'd gone above his investigations and was going to help some of the workers with childcare? Her Aunt Wendy could have used that twenty years ago.

"Thank you for telling me that. It eases a lot of my worries for the people of this town and for my own selfish wants." She gave him a quick smile before the girl from the other day popped into her mind. "Is Sage your girlfriend?"

He jerked back at that, and Kassidy held her breath,

waiting for his answer. "Sage Cutler? No, a thousand times no. I took her on one date to a charity auction." He paused a moment. "No, the person I want to be my girlfriend is you, Kassidy McBride."

It took a few extra seconds for her mind to wrap around those words. Her head whipped in his direction to make sure he wasn't just teasing her.

"You want me to be your girlfriend?"

He grinned, nodding. "Kassidy, I know we've had plenty of differences, but you are the person I want to be with. I know, you've thought I was heartless to think about closing down a plant where most of the town is employed, but it takes time to make the big decisions, and I really wanted it to work. My grandfather always taught me to look at it from all angles before disrupting people's lives, and I made sure to step into a few people's shoes, so to speak, before I made that decision. It was all because of you." He gave her a quick smile and focused back on the horses, guiding them around the path the two of them had come up with the week before.

Kassidy laughed. "I overheard your grandmother say something to Margritte a few days ago about you working the machines."

"And I was sore for two days after." His laughter died down to a somber expression. "This past week with you not talking to me has been one of the worst of my life. When I'm with you, I can relax, have fun, and not worry so much about failing as the CEO of my company."

"I guess we all worry about failing somewhat. I was beginning to wonder if I'd ever figure out life, because I thought it should just be like barrel racing. Put in the time and the work and I would automatically be successful. But failure isn't the end of the road, right? Just like you told me at the bank."

Dustin smiled and nodded. "I'm surprised you remembered that."

"I remember a lot of what you've said. This job has given me the chance to test my talents, and I'm so grateful for that."

"Thank you for making Christmas fun again. That's saying a lot with all that's happened to me around Christmas." His expression sobered. "So, I guess what I'm saying is that I like you, Kassidy, maybe even love you at this point. But if you don't feel the same, then—"

Kassidy leaned forward, and instead of responding with words, she pressed her lips to his. It was everything she'd ever imagined it would be, times a hundred. If only her teenage self could see her now.

When they pulled apart, trying to catch their breath, he gave her a one-sided grin. "So I take that as a yes?"

"Of course, Dustin Wakefield. I would love to be your girlfriend."

EPILOGUE

The year had flown, and here Kassidy was, just finishing up another gala at Wakefield Mansion. She'd spent even more time there since the last Christmas after Dustin decided to move back to Coldwater Creek permanently and run the company from there. He had to leave on business a couple times a month, but when she wasn't planning one of the many events the townspeople of Coldwater Creek were clamoring for her to do, she went with him.

She was grateful she hadn't caved before the gala last year and gone back to riding. Racing was a great part of her past, but event planning and dating Dustin were her future. Sometimes she still geeked out over that fact.

With presents wrapped and work on hold until after Christmas, she was ready for a nice, hot bubble bath.

The last package she'd been waiting for arrived on December twenty-third, and she carefully unwrapped the small green ornament, hanging it on one of the front-facing boughs of the Christmas tree.

"What is that?" Hunter asked over her shoulder.

She swatted him away and picked up her phone to text Dustin. *Party is starting in ten minutes. Are you on your way?*

The doorbell rang a few minutes later and in walked Dustin, his arm looped with Grandma Grace, and trailed by Walker and Lauren. Kassidy did everything she could to not think about the ornament on the tree while they ate. She wanted it to be a surprise for him, but it was proving hard to wait as her mom and dad kept talking. Once dinner was finished and the dishes were cleaned, they all moved into the family room.

Hunter went to turn on the Christmas lights, rolling his eyes at Kassidy as he saw the ornament again. Maybe, once he got the meaning of the ornament, he'd be a little more sensitive.

She couldn't keep her legs from bouncing up and down, trying not to give away the hunt too easily. Because of the gala, the McBrides had moved their traditional Christmas Eve celebrations to the night before, since they'd been invited to attend this year, along with the rest of Coldwater Creek.

When the last early present had been opened, she settled in next to Dustin, hoping he wouldn't notice how fast her heart was beating.

Dustin ran his fingers through her hair, the two of them watching Baby Emmy, Easton and Natalie's ten-month-old, crawl around playing with the Christmas wrapping paper. At one point he paused.

"What's that?" he asked, pointing toward the tree.

Kassidy pretended she couldn't see anything, and he finally stood, striding toward the Christmas tree. He gently pulled back a few of the boughs.

When he turned, he held up the glass pickle ornament by the ribbon. "Did you get this?" he asked, staring at Kassidy.

As she gave a quick nod, tears pricked her eyes when she saw the struggle of emotions across his face. He stepped forward, pulling her into a tight embrace. "Thank you. Thank you for remembering this."

When he let go and stepped back, she said, "Do you want your extra present?" She could see the small package of caramel-apple suckers she'd wrapped a few days before in preparation for this.

"What is with the pickle?" Colter asked loudly.

"Shhh!" the rest of the room said, each of them riveted on the scene in front of them.

Dustin grinned. "If it's all right, I want to give you the extra present this time."

Kneeling on one knee, he opened a small velvet box. "Kassidy Tonya McBride, you've been a whirlwind in my life, making sure that I keep living it. You've helped me see that I can love my job and still get out and be a normal human being. I love how you complement me and how you won't let me get away with doing things halfway." He paused, swallowing with effort. When he spoke, his voice was husky. "Will you be my wife?"

She couldn't hold back the tears anymore, and they rolled freely down her cheeks. She gathered him up in her arms and held on tight as her family cheered.

"Thank you for what's been a whirlwind of a year. For taking a chance on me as an event planner, and then again as your girlfriend. If our future is anything like this past year, we'll conquer it together." Emotion surged to her throat, making it difficult to speak. When she did, she said in a whisper, "Of course, I'll marry you, Dustin Wakefield."

* * *

Love small-town romance? Keep reading for a sneak peak of Becca & Colton's story in Love Under Construction

* * *

Thank you for reading *Love in the Details!* If you enjoyed it, I would love to see a review from you. You can also subscribe to Britney's newsletter here:
Subscribe to Britney's List

LOVE UNDER CONSTRUCTION

Becca Taylor's morning wasn't going as planned. After waking up late, her hair wouldn't cooperate into the usual soft curls she liked. And there was almost nothing she could do for the puffiness under her eyes after a long night of nightmares.

As she heated her oatmeal in the microwave, Becca's mind glossed over the memories that kept recurring in her mind, the ones where she pictured her parents' and brother's deaths after sliding off a cliff in their car. The images that kept her bound to Sage Creek.

She'd been dressed in her graduation cap and gown, ready to receive the certificate for her bachelor's degree, and it was the moment her carefree and adventurous life had come to a halt. She knew it, and yet the ability to break away from her rigid routine was something she struggled with.

Control was the name of the game, and most days she conquered. But not today.

Glancing down at her blouse, she glared at the glob of warm oatmeal she'd just dropped that was now seeping through. Another outfit change was not what she had in mind. The clock told her she was already ten minutes late leaving the house. The thought of her tardiness caused that familiar knot to form in her stomach.

Since the accident, being late was something Becca hated. Her father, who'd grown up in a military family, had often wanted to strangle her as a teenager as she arrived when she was ready. But now, even five and a half years after his death, she remembered his words and stuck by them almost religiously.

The measure of a person is noted in their appreciation of time, especially the time of others.

She didn't necessarily have anyone waiting on her at the moment, as her flower shop opened in twenty minutes, but the fact was she was all about routine and order, not change. When that routine was thrown, it seemed as though everything went with it.

What if something life-threatening happened because she was late? It was the one thing she wished she could change about that day so long ago. That on the one day her parents had left late, they would've been able to avoid the car which had been speeding past, clipping the back bumper.

"It'll be all right, Becca," she tried to tell herself, pushing the thoughts from her mind.

She changed her shirt, opting for a short-sleeved one with a sweater over top. At least if she spilled again, she could remove the top layer. Her makeup would have to go on at the shop. She'd only see Karla, the town coffee shop owner, before then, and she could handle that.

Running outside, Becca lengthened her stride, passing her flower shop and coming to the corner of the street in seconds before turning south onto Main Street. She loved living next to the shop, making it easier to bring flowers from her garden out back into the back room once they were ready.

The fact that the coffee shop was only two units down from her place made it even sweeter. The benefit of living in a small town, as compared to the large city where she'd gone to college, was that most things were in walking distance.

She glanced back, breathing a sigh of relief as she didn't see many people walking along the street, until she hit something hard, knocking her backward and almost onto her backside.

As she felt the momentum take her one way, a warm hand caught her wrist, stopping her fall and pulling her back up and off her feet. With her head buried in the flannel shirt of her rescuer, Becca wondered if this day could get any worse.

Stepping back, she glanced up, arching her head more than normal. Sure, she was only five foot four, but she felt as if she was looking sky-high at the brown-haired, brown-eyed vision standing before her. Her heart thumped as her eyes focused even more, and the similarities between him and another man from her past sent the adrenaline rushing through her.

"I'm so sorry. It's been a morning." She glanced at her shoes, realizing that although both shoes were black, they were different patterns. Groaning inwardly, she looked back up, sweeping back a section of her hair. "Thank you for, um, saving me from total embarrassment."

She took a step to the side, hoping to continue her path around him. She didn't need to think about her ex-fiancé on top of everything that had already gone wrong today.

"Not a problem. Glad I could be of assistance, Miss—" He held out his hand, his eyebrows near his hairline.

She stopped, trying to be polite while guarding her heart from the memories that flashed in her mind. "Taylor. Becca Taylor. Who are you?"

He smiled, accentuating a scar on the side of his chin. "Colton Maxfield. I just arrived last night, but this little town seems…nice." The forced compliment caused Becca to frown. She'd had her fair share of people downing the small town over the years, and from that history, they didn't usually stick around long.

"Well, I hope we can convince you that we really are *nice*, Mr. Maxfield. It was nice to meet you, but I'm late." She nodded and skirted around the side of him, making a beeline for the coffee shop at the end of the block. As she walked in, the line stretched back to the door, and Becca ground her teeth together.

"Becca!" a voice called from behind the counter. Karla had spotted her and waved her forward. "What happened to you this morning? Your tea is probably cold by now." The older woman handed her a cup, and while it wasn't as steaming hot as usual, it was still quite warm.

"Thank you, Karla. Long night, and I slept in. But things are looking up now that I have this." Becca grinned as she lifted the cup a few inches. She took a sip, feeling some of the tension seep away. "You are a lifesaver. Remind me about this when you need flowers."

Karla chuckled and nodded. "Will do, girl. Better get going. I know how you are with your schedule."

Becca turned, waving to just about everyone in line as she moved past. She turned right once outside and walked back to her flower shop. Pulling out her key, she opened the door and breathed in the smell of the flowers, something that never seemed to grow old no matter how long she'd owned the store.

"Morning, Becca," Carissa said once Becca made it to the back room. She was a high school junior who'd been working at the shop for several months now. Having her there was fun because Becca got to be boss and teacher at the same time, and with how fast Carissa picked things up, it took some of the pressure off Becca.

"Good morning, Carissa. I didn't expect you in so early today." Becca dropped her things onto the large table next to the wall and pulled on an apron from the same area.

Carissa nodded. "It was one of those teacher prep days. I figured I'd come in since we have that big order coming up for the wedding this Saturday. Do you need me to order more lilies?"

Glancing over at the large cooler where most of the flowers were stored, Becca mentally went over the number of flowers they'd need. "I ordered a bunch to come in on Thursday, but it might be good to double-check so we aren't scrambling right before the wedding."

"Are you all right, Becca?" Carissa's eyebrows were scrunched together with concern.

Becca hadn't realized she was twisting her fingers together, causing the knuckles to turn white against her already pale skin.

"I'm fine. I just feel off today." She thought about the events of the morning again, and the picture of the handsome stranger popped into her mind. "Do you know a Colton Maxfield?"

Carissa put down the scissors as she picked up several already cut stems, placing them in a box. "I've heard of him. He got in last night and stayed at the hotel. Mom checked him in."

Carissa's mother, Delia, had owned and managed the hotel since her husband died two years earlier from cancer. The woman worked hard but was the source of gossip in the small town. She knew a lot of what was going to happen before it did, so of course she knew the new guy in town.

"How long is he here for?" Becca asked, trying to be casual. She didn't need people thinking she'd taken an interest in the stranger, because her heart was still locked up, not ready to attempt love again. The last thing she needed was the pity blind dates the women of this town could contrive at a moment's notice.

"I think quite a while. Mom said something about him working on that new development down the road. I guess they're putting in a bunch of townhomes and apartments?" Carissa leaned over the table, filling out the paper for the order she'd just boxed up, not really showing any emotion when it came to the development.

Becca felt enough for her anyway. She'd been elected to the city council the year before, and she loved every minute of the politics and helping make decisions that impacted the town. This was one decision that still hurt.

She and Richard Lawson were the only ones to vote against a preliminary meeting to look into the development, thinking that by bringing in the smaller housing on the south end of town, they would be changing the dynamic of the town. And if there was one thing Becca didn't like, it was change, of any sort. Change only brought heartache and a lack of control, the kind that lasted far after the events had taken place.

She thought back to the man on the street and realized she should have guessed he was some kind of builder. Her ex-fiancé had been one too, and while he typically wore suits to work, there was a certain confidence about contractors that she should have seen despite the flannel shirt Colton wore earlier.

Taking a few minutes to put on her makeup, Becca tried to get the image of the man out of her head. The commonalities between him and her ex-fiancé, just from a two-minute conversation, were throwing her brain for a loop. And if he was going to be staying in town for several weeks, how was she going to avoid him?

Shaking her head, she put her makeup bag back into her purse and focused on the list of orders that had come in at the end of yesterday. Sorting through the flowers that had been delivered that morning, she tried to find the ones she needed, all the while pushing thoughts of her past to the background. She hadn't had so many memories come to the surface in months, and it took several focused distractions to finally help the tension in her body ease up.

A few hours later, Becca walked into the main room of her flower shop, bringing two vases of tulips to sit in the front cooler. The store had been busy that morning but had slowed down for the afternoon rush. She'd dropped off the weekly orders around town and then came back to relieve Carissa, grateful for all she'd done to help get the orders ready before leaving for the day.

The break in customers was nice because as much as she loved flowers, holidays seemed to kick everything up a notch, even in the small town of Sage Creek. With the Founder's Day Festival two weeks away, she knew the two days before would be the most stressful of the year, trying to get all the flowers in, cut, and arranged.

She couldn't imagine living anywhere but this quaint town, nestled as it was in the mountains of western Colorado. She'd grown up in Sage Creek, only leaving to earn a degree. The minute she got to school in Salt Lake, she'd realized that there really was no place like home. The bustling city, while exhilarating and fun in many respects, now seemed tainted by the death of her family. Her small town provided just about everything she needed, and things were predictable, helping to keep her anxiety to a minimum.

After the three and a half years it took to get a bachelor's degree in interior design, her plan had been to stay in the city, interning for a popular designer. But the safe haven of Sage Creek had been the balm to her soul once she'd been able to stop the tears from falling. She'd opened up her flower shop and decided this was where she'd stay. A place of low crime and low risk made life bearable.

The doorbell chimed, and she looked up with a ready smile to see the mayor walk in.

"Mayor Watkins. What a surprise. Was there something wrong with this week's order? I just dropped it by Town Hall a couple of hours ago." She closed the door to the storage case and rested her hands on her hips.

The old man chuckled. "No, nothing was wrong. The women have all been ogling it. I'm actually here on personal business." He grimaced. "I need something for Dottie. I forgot that it's our half-something today, and I'm already in trouble for forgetting."

Becca grinned. "Half what?"

"I'm not really sure. That woman keeps track of every date and every first of everything, which is why I'm in the doghouse most of the time. I figured some flowers would smooth it over." He rolled his eyes and shook his head as he smiled, causing Becca to laugh.

A picture of the mayor's wife popped into her head. For the most part, Becca expected people with white hair to be sweet and full of wisdom. Dorothy Watkins could be just that at times, but she was a firecracker for the most part, and it was easier to stay on her good side rather than to have to win her back over. But then again, she and the mayor had been married over forty years now, having celebrated the milestone the year before in a big town party. The two of them were like surrogate grandparents, and she was grateful for all they did for her.

"A couple of lilies, then? I know they're her favorite."

The mayor pointed at her. "See, this is why I come to you. You know just about everything about everyone in this town, especially their favorite flowers. Can you wrap them in some paper so I can take them?"

"Of course. Let me run back and get some for you." Becca strode into the back room and pulled some fresh lilies from the cooler. She didn't want Mrs. Watkins to have anything to complain about, even a small brown spot on a petal. If there was one good source of free advertising for Becca in this town, it was the fact that when Mayor Watkins bought his wife flowers, she told the world.

Not that Becca had any competition, being the only flower place around, but it was still nice to nudge people her way. When the townspeople's budgets grew tighter, money for flowers was put on hold, and she appreciated all the business she could get from this small town.

Resuming her spot out front, she rolled the few flowers in some tissue paper and tied them with a pink ribbon. Typing the figures into the cash register, she looked up and asked, "Cash or card?"

"Cash." He handed her a twenty-dollar bill. "I'll get these home before the council meeting tonight. You'll be there, right?"

"I wouldn't miss it. I hear we've got some interesting items on the agenda." She raised her eyebrows and grinned. Again, the handsome stranger popped into her mind, causing her to wonder what was wrong with her brain and its fixation with the builder.

"Yeah. That new subdivision has caused quite the ruckus. But we'll figure it out, right? That's what we always do in this town. We may argue for a little bit, but when we make a decision, we put the past behind us."

"That right there is one of the reasons I'm still here, Mayor. Putting the past behind us and moving on." Several different thoughts clouded her mind at once, and she had to push them away, focusing on the present before her. "I'll see you tonight."

She handed him the bouquet of flowers and went back to

cleaning up, her thoughts drifting to how building would impact the town.

The mayor had talked her ear off about the subdivision two nights before when Dorothy had invited her over for dinner. He was in favor of the growth, but for all of the reasons he thought it would be good, Becca just shook her head and hoped it wouldn't go through.

The contractor was trying to build thirty homes, along with several apartment buildings. Although it wouldn't double the population of the town, it would significantly impact it. The thought of outsiders—people who didn't share the same vision as the people of Sage Creek—disrupting the dynamic made Becca worry.

Tonight's weekly Wednesday meeting would be interesting, that was for sure. It wasn't some big theater production or sporting event, but sometimes she was tempted to bring a bag of popcorn and watch as the petty drama unfolded. Peter would've laughed at that thought, because what excited him were city lights and thousands of people. Something she should have noticed long before he disappeared.

Shaking her head, Becca pushed thoughts of her ex-fiancé away, knowing she had to forget about him at some point. She'd worry about the forever later and hope that the small things would take over the ache she still felt from their breakup a year and a half before.

* * *

To KEEP READING *Love Under Construction, grab it here.*

Loving His Reporter Girl

* * *

Join Britney's newsletter

Get the latest updates on new releases and other fun tidbits!

ABOUT THE AUTHOR

Britney Mills was born in Utah but parts of her heart lie in Boston, Washington D.C. and Germany. Her love of writing began with the third grade book her teacher assigned her to write and she spent hours hidden behind her mother's couch writing pages and pages about knights and castles. Now she writes about romance. Go figure.

When she's not mothering her five small children, writing or reading, she's probably out playing a sport, going on a hike, or binge watching a murder mystery series. The way to her heart is through homemade chocolate chip cookies and five minutes peace.